Magic From the Dark

Judy Lunsford

Published by Judy Lunsford, 2021.

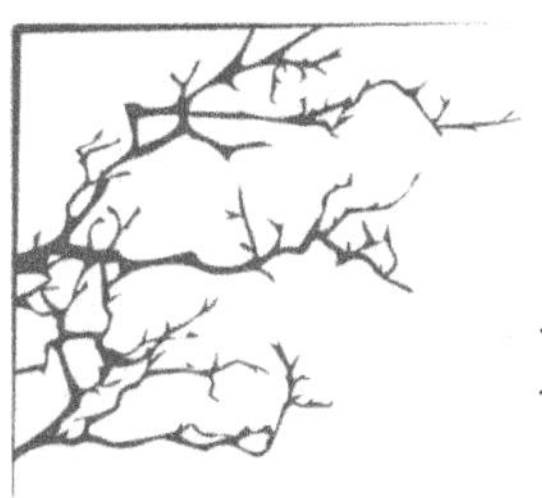

Introduction

This short story collection is filled with stories written mostly in 2020 and 2021. The stories are filled with hints of dark magic, some of which were probably inspired by the feelings of dread that accompanied the COVID pandemic shutdown.

Included in this collection are flash fiction stories as well as much longer stories.

I love writing stories that have the battle ongoing between the darkness and the light that resides within us all. And each story deals with the main character's battle between the two opposing forces.

I hope you find something you like.

Happy reading!

JUDY LUNSFORD
September 2021

PLANTMAN662

1

RAMONA LOOKED OUT OVER the balcony and stared at the city beneath her. She missed the green grass of her old house. She had spent hundreds of hours tending to the garden that it used to overlook. There wasn't another building for miles. Just lush green and fragrant colorful flowers.

Here in the city, there was nothing but buildings. No gardens, no grass, very few trees. And the smell was anything but good.

She stared at her little balcony garden and watched the leaves of her tiny sprouts wavering in the breeze. She hoped that one day, her little garden would become a green wall, separating her from the horrific view of the city and give her a small sense of the peace she had in her lush garden before.

Mona loved two things. Her garden and her horse, Mia. It had broken her heart when her parents told her they were going to have to sell Mia because they wouldn't be able to afford the monthly cost of boarding her. They promised Mona she could do whatever she wanted with the money from the sale of her beloved horse.

Her mother had let her take over their apartment's tiny balcony. Mona got some long planters and various colorful clay pots that she had filled with seedlings and soil and put it out on the balcony. She also brought with her a few of the plants she thought she could uproot and bring with her in pots, so she didn't have to start from seeds. Her mother was working two jobs to maintain their tiny one-bedroom apartment, so she wouldn't have much time to use the balcony anyways.

Mona made the balcony into her one place that was truly hers. The one place where she might find sanctuary from this now horrible life. A life in the city, without her father, where her mother had to work day and night to support the two of them.

Mona was relegated to sleeping on the sofa in the living room, so her mother conceded the balcony to Mona easily, in hopes of repairing the damage moving to the city and losing the privacy of her own room had done to their relationship.

The balcony was tiny, but Mona considered it "her room." Mona sat in front of her planter boxes even though there was barely enough room to sit on the tiny balcony amongst all of the planters and pots.

Mona could smell the scent of the potting soil over the smell of the city. It brought a smile to her face, in spite of the view.

"Mona, come here, please," her mother called from the kitchen.

Reluctantly, Mona got up and went inside.

"I want you to make sure you do your homework tonight," her mother said, as she wiped down their tiny kitchen counter. "I put some dinner in the fridge for you, make sure you eat it."

Mona nodded as she watched her mother. It had only been six months since her father left, but Mona noticed that her mother looked ten years older. She didn't remember her mother looking so old back home in their old house. She had looked young and vi-brant. But she hadn't had to hold down two jobs to pay the rent. She also hadn't had to raise Mona by herself at the time.

Mona hated her father for what he had done. The lies were the worst. When Mona and her mother found out that her father had a second family, it was devastating enough. When he told them that he was leaving them to go live with the second family, she wasn't sure her mother would ever recover. She wasn't sure that she would ever recover.

Her mother sighed and came over and leaned on the other side of the tiny breakfast bar that Mona was leaning on and staring blankly into the kitchen.

Mona knew what her mother was going to ask next.

"Have you made your decision yet?" she asked.

Mona shook her head no.

"Technically, she is your sister," her mother said. "If you want to meet her, I won't have a problem with it."

"Are you sure?" Mona asked.

"I'm positive," her mother said hesitantly. "We may not like what your father did, but that's not Silvia's fault."

"If I went to meet her," Mona asked. "Would you come with me?"

Mona stared into her mother's sad blue eyes for a few moments while her mother pondered the question. She could see the answer forming before her mother spoke.

"I don't know that I am ready for that step just yet," her mother finally answered.

"I don't know how ready I am either," Mona sighed.

"Just remember," her mother reached out and held Mona's hand. "None of this is your fault. None of this is Silvia's fault either.

You two are the innocent parties in this. And if you two want to be friends, even sisters, that is fine. Healthy even. You two have a common trauma in this. You could help each other through all of this mess."

Mona nodded.

She hadn't thought about the fact that Silvia could be as mad at her father, their father, as she was. That there was the possibility that she and this stranger could bond over a common enemy. Their lying, cheating father. But there was also the possibility that this sister could choose her dad over Mona. That she would be happy to be the chosen daughter.

It was Silvia who had asked to meet Mona. Would she have asked to meet her sister if she had meant it to be a hostile meeting? Or was she just curious to meet her older sister?

Mona thought about the age difference. It was only three years. Her father had been cheating and lying for over 13 years. At least. That was most of her life. She felt betrayed that he had lied for that long. He had hidden this other life. He had done it so successfully. Mona and her mother never had a clue. His business trips seemed legitimate. It wasn't until recently that they found out that he never had to travel for his job.

"I'll be working late tonight," her mother's voice interrupted Mona's thoughts. "Make sure you go to bed at a reasonable hour. I love you."

Mona nodded as her mother grabbed her purse and ran over to kiss Mona on the temple.

"And remember to do your homework," her mother called over her shoulder as she ran out the front door.

Mona reached into her backpack, which she had left sitting on the counter when she went outside to the balcony to visit her plants after school. She unzipped the front pocket and pulled out the small pink envelope that she had been carrying with her for the last few days.

The perfect handwriting on the front intrigued her. It was so meticulous in a time where a lot of schools weren't teaching much cursive anymore. The letter inside had the same perfect script. Written on pink stationery with a purple pen was the letter that her little sister had written her. It was short and simple. She wanted to meet her big sister. Silvia was 12 years old and had always wanted a big sister. Mona, at 15, had been her dream come true. Despite what their father had done, could they please meet?

Mona had read the letter over and over again. She had to admit that she had always wanted a sister herself. She also had to admit that her curiosity was getting the better of her.

She decided she wanted to meet her little sister.

* 2 *

Mona hesitated at the front door. Her hand hovered in front of the blue apartment door with 137 in gold plated door numbers nailed to it, her fingers curled under to knock. But she couldn't bring herself to do it.

She had come all the way across town to meet her little sister, but now that she was here, she couldn't bring herself to knock.

Before she could change her mind, the door opened. Mona caught her breath as she saw her little sister for the first time.

She had golden blonde hair and eyes to match. Mona had never seen eyes that color before. They were striking. Her pale white skin made the golden eyes stand out all the more. It reminded Mona of a cat that once used to frequent her yard back at her old house.

"Hi," the girl said. "I'm Silvia. You must be Mona."

She smiled widely at Mona.

Mona was too shocked to react. She still had one hand raised in the air to knock on the now open door.

"Come in," Silvia grabbed Mona's hand and dragged her inside, and shut the door behind them.

The living room was ordinary. Mona didn't know why she was expecting something extravagant. Everything was in shades of red, which was her father's favorite color. Red walls, red sofa, red drapes, red pictures hung on the walls with red frames. Even the furniture was made from a dark red cherrywood. The reds were something her mother fought against, because too much red made her feel agitated and angry. Mona could feel the same thing, although she didn't know if it was the red, or the fact that she was standing in a living room that has belonged to her father for much longer than Mona had been away from their old house. This was their home. The other family. They had lived here for years.

"Come with me," Silvia pulled Mona away from all of the horrible shades of red. "I hate the living room."

Mona let herself be led down a small hallway and into Silvia's room.

It was a stark contrast to the angry reds of the living room.

The walls were painted a bright sunshine yellow and the furniture was all white. What caught Mona's attention was all of the plants. They were everywhere.

Mona wandered around the room looking at all of the plants. There were pansies and African violets sitting on the window sill. There were hanging plants of all kinds dangling from a bar that was mounted across the room in front of the window. The view of the city obscured by the wall of green that hung down with long arms to strangle the ugliness outside.

There were plants on every surface of the room. Small plants in pots sat on top of her dresser and on shelves of her bookcase. Mona ran her fingers along the delicate strands of English Ivy that trailed down one side of the bookcase, all the way to the floor. There were larger plants in big pots in the corners of the room, each plant in the perfect spot for how much light they tend to like.

"You like plants?" Silvia asked hopefully.

"I love them," Mona whispered. "I have a balcony that I am trying to fill."

"If you want any cuttings, you're welcome to them," Silvia said, standing uncomfortably close to Mona as she spoke.

Mona stepped back to look at her little sister. She hadn't expected to have anything in common with her sister but their father. She wasn't expecting this. The last thing she expected was to share a common love with her sister. Or to have something so bonding as sharing cuttings from her plants.

"I would like that," Mona said. She couldn't get over the yellow of her sister's eyes. It was creepy, almost alien. "You can have any cuttings from mine as well. Although I don't have a lot at this point."

"Did you bring any plants with you from your old house?" Silvia asked hopefully.

"Yes," Mona answered. "A few."

"Maybe I'd like a cutting from one of those," Silvia said. "Something that's been with you for a long time."

Mona nodded. She stared into the golden eyes that seemed to bore right through her and into her soul. "Sure, if you'd like."

Silvia broke eye contact and walked over to one of the plants by the huge bright window. "I'll give you a cutting of this one, it's my favorite."

Mona walked over to the window and looked at the plant. It was nothing like anything she had ever seen before.

"What is it?" she asked.

Silvia shrugged, "I don't know what it's called." She clipped a bit off the side, where the plant seemed to be growing wildly. "I love it though, see how it just seems to capture the light in its leaves?"

Mona stared at the clipping and stared in amazement as the veins in the leaves seemed to almost glow in the sunlight.

"It's a beautiful plant," Mona whispered.

"Take it," Silvia said. "It loves sunlight and lots of water."

"You don't know what it is?" Mona asked as she put her hand out for the clipping.

Silvia shook her head. "I can't find it in any of my plant books, or on any of my resources on the computer. It's a mystery." She shrugged as if it didn't matter.

"Maybe I'll have some luck looking it up," Mona said.

"Good luck," Silvia shrugged.

Mona stared at the cutting in the palm of her hand. She cradled it like it was the most precious thing in the world and stared at it as if it held her in a trance.

"You okay?" her little sister asked.

"Yeah," Mona looked up into the golden eyes of her sister. "Yeah, I'm fine."

"Do you want something to carry that home in?" her sister asked.

"No," Mona shook her head. "I'm going straight home. In fact, I should be going."

"Already?" Silvia whined. "But you just got here. I was going to make us a snack."

Mona shook her head, "No, thank you. I really have to go home and get some homework done. I just stopped by to meet you. That's all."

"You'll come back?" Silvia asked.

Mona nodded. "Yes, I'll come back. We have more in common than I thought we would."

Silvia smiled in relief. "You're welcome here any time."

"Thank you," Mona said.

"I'm going to love having a sister," Silvia said. "Are you sure you don't want me to make you something to eat before you go?"

"No, thanks," Mona said. "I promised my mom I wouldn't stay long for the first visit. I think this is a little hard on her."

"Oh yeah," Silvia looked at the floor. "I sort of forgot about that part."

"I didn't," Mona said.

Silvia looked hurt. She lifted her wide golden eyes towards Mona and they were filled with tears.

"You won't let that stop you from coming back, will you?" Silvia asked, with a slight quiver in her voice.

"No," Mona shook her head. "That won't stop me from coming back. You're my sister."

Silvia wiped her eyes in relief and smiled again. "Then maybe you'll come back again this week?"

"Sure," Mona nodded. "I'll be back in a few days. Maybe on the weekend."

Silvia seemed happy with the plans and showed Mona out.

Once outside the door, Mona looked closely at the plant cutting that sat in the palm of her hand as she waited for the elevator. There was no sunlight in the hallway, but the veins in the leaves still seemed to have a faint glow to them.

Mona squinted at the cutting and felt drawn to the little plant. She couldn't put her finger on why it was so intriguing. Maybe because neither girl could seem to identify it. Mona was anxious to get home and try to figure it out for herself so she could be the one to tell her little sister what the plant's name was.

* 3 *

Mona tended to the little cutting she had brought home with her immediately. She hoped the trip home hadn't made it so that the cutting would have a difficult time sprouting and taking root. She had a few small terra cotta pots left, so she filled it with moist soil and put the cutting into it.

She remembered what her sister said about it liking sunlight and water, so she made extra sure that the soil was thoroughly wet.

Mona then sat down at the laptop she and her mother shared and started looking up plants on her favorite websites. She scrolled through hundreds of pictures of plants and even studied hybrids.

After hours of looking, she still had found nothing on the cutting from her sister.

Mona took a few pictures with her phone and loaded them into a few plant forums, so see if anyone else could identify her plant. After feeling like she had done all she could do, she looked at the clock on her phone.

It was late. She still hadn't eaten dinner or gotten to her homework. Mona headed to the refrigerator and took out the dinner her mother had left her. She popped it into the microwave and looked at her homework while she waited.

She didn't have much. It was still very close to the beginning of the school year and so the teachers hadn't started piling on the assignments yet. The computer made a pinging noise from the website she was still logged into. She went over to check her messages for the forum.

There was one reply to the picture she had posted of her sister's cutting.

It read, "GET RID OF IT!" from PlantMan662.

The microwave beeped over her shoulder in the kitchen to signal it was finished.

Mona ignored it and started typing her response.

"Why? Is it poisonous?"

Moments later, the response came back in a private message, "Much worse. Where did you get it?"

Mona ignored her dinner once again as she sat down and wrote back, "From my sister. What would be worse than poisonous?"

"Where did your sister get it?"

Mona continued the conversation with PlantMan662 and revealed that she had just met her sister that very day and that her sister had it growing in her bedroom and had given her the cutting because it was her favorite plant.

She asked again what could be worse than poison.

There was a long pause before he replied again.

"Did you notice anything strange about your sister?" PlantMan662 asked.

Mona paused before writing, "She has yellow eyes. Like a cat."

"Don't go back to see her. Throw away the cutting. Down the garbage disposal," PlantMan662 responded.

"Why?" Mona typed back.

After another long pause, which seemed like forever to Mona, PlantMan662 answered back, "She's fae. Probably a changeling. She wants to kidnap you."

"She's what???" Mona replied.

PlantMan662 had logged off.

4

Mona spent the rest of the evening on the internet. She looked up everything she could about fae and changelings. She sat at the kitchen counter with the laptop glowing in the darkness, her dinner still uneaten in the microwave.

Her mother came home from work well after midnight, and she found Mona still deep in research on the computer.

"What are you doing?" her mother asked.

Mona quickly closed the laptop. "I was just doing some research."

Mona's mother opened the microwave that was blinking END in the dark kitchen. "You didn't eat your dinner."

"I must've forgot," Mona muttered. "I was just really into my homework."

"Well, did you at least finish that?" her mother asked as she pulled the plate out of the microwave and gave the cold food a poke with her index finger.

"Mostly," Mona said. "There's still some research I'd like to get done."

"What class?" her mother asked, trashing the food on the plate.

"Uh, science," Mona lied.

"Well, will you at least eat a bowl of cereal and go to bed within an hour?" her mother asked.

"Yeah," Mona nodded. "I promise."

"Ok," her mother kissed Mona's forehead as she walked past her towards her room. "I'm beat. I have to get up early. So, I'm going to bed. Make sure you're not far behind me."

"Ok, I promise," Mona said. "Good night."

"Good night," her mother said as she shut her bedroom door.

Mona stared into the darkness where her mother had disappeared into her room. She hated that her mother had to work so many hours. She hated that they had to live in the city, instead of their nice home on a big piece of property. She knew her mother hated it as well, but that she did what she had to do.

Mona couldn't let anything else bad happen to her family.

She opened the computer again and stared at the website she had been reading.

It described different legends about changelings.

Mona found the whole idea of fae being real to be ridiculous. But the more she read about the different legends from around the world and how similar some of them seemed, the more she thought that there could be the possibility of them being real.

She shook her head and thought she was being crazy from being overtired and decided it was time to get some sleep.

Mona walked over to the couch and laid down. She had forgotten to eat some cereal, and her homework remained undone.

Mona's mind reeled with the images from the internet and she fell asleep dreaming about changelings and fae.

* 5 *

Mona woke up the next morning to find that her mother had already left for work.

She stumbled off of the couch and untangled herself from the purple and blue crocheted afghan her mother must have put over her before she left for her day job.

Mona staggered to the kitchen, rubbing the sleep from her eyes. She found a pot of hot coffee and a note from her mother stuck to the coffee maker.

It simply said, "EAT BREAKFAST!"

Mona reached up into the cabinet above the coffee maker and pulled down a mug and a bowl.

She first filled the mug with coffee and added cream and sugar to it. She inhaled the welcoming scent of the first coffee of the morning and took a sip. She then grabbed a box of cereal out of the pantry and put some in a bowl. After adding some milk, she grabbed a spoon and started to eat.

She hadn't realized how hungry she was until she had started eating. She wound up pouring more cereal into the milk that was left in the bottom of the bowl and ate her second helping just as fast as the first.

She put her bowl in the sink and grabbed her coffee and headed out onto her little balcony.

The sun was already up and was peeking out at her from between the buildings that blocked her view of the sky. Mona sighed and sat down in front of her planter boxes. She looked over at the cutting from Silvia and almost dropped her mug.

The single cutting had tripled in size overnight. It was no longer the tiny little cutting that it was the day before. It was now a lush healthy small plant. Mona reached for it and pulled it gently away from the soil. Instead of popping right out like a new cutting would, a solid root system held the plant in place in the pot. Mona used her fingers to clear away some of the dirt to make sure. There was a full root system already established in the pot.

Mona let go of the plant and immediately went inside and washed her hands. She still didn't know what kind of plant it was, and she didn't know what it might do to her. PlantMan662 didn't seem so crazy to her anymore.

Mona went over to her computer and logged back into the forum where she had met PlantMan662. She typed in a private message telling him about the plant's growth and then waited.

She continued researching plants and fae until, a few hours later, PlantMan662 responded to her message.

"I told you to put it down the garbage disposal," PlantMan662 replied. "Now it might be too late."

"Why would it be too late?" she asked.

"Because now it has roots," PlantMan662 responded. "It's more difficult to destroy if it has roots."

"What do I do with it?" she asked.

"Do you have a fireplace?" he asked.

"No," she replied.

"Find a place to burn it," he said. "Carefully. And watch the roots."

Mona logged off and went out to look at the plant once again. It was impossible for it to have grown as much as it had overnight. The plant seemed to glow more brightly in the rising sunlight.

Mona couldn't get her mind off of all of the information she had read on the web about fae and changelings. They were dangerous. They were not to be toyed with. They were not friends. Even if it happened to be her sister.

Mona thought for a moment. If her sister was a changeling, that meant that Silvia wasn't really her sister. Her sister was out there somewhere, kidnapped by fairies.

Mona shook her head again. How could she possibly believe in fairies? She was a teenager. She didn't believe in fairies any more.

She stared down at the plant in the pot and still couldn't get over how large it had become in less than 12 hours.

Mona went over to the couch and put on her shoes. She went out to the balcony and picked up the pot. She got some matches out of the kitchen and put them in her jeans pocket. Then she carried the pot down into the basement.

She had only been in the basement of the building once before. The super had showed it to her mother just before they moved in and told them that they could store extra belongings down there. He had locking cages to keep people's things separate and safe.

There was also a concrete floor and extra cleaning supplies stored down there. Mona remembered the smell of bleach and other cleaners and they burned her throat while she was down there. She vowed that none of her stuff would be stored there because she didn't want any of her belongings to smell like cleaning fluids.

Mona found a metal bucket that was with the cleaning supplies and some newspaper that had been tossed in a corner. As she walked to the door, she saw a bottle of lighter fluid up on a shelf and grabbed that too.

She took everything outside, back near the dumpsters in the alleyway behind the building and pulled the plant out of the pot. She put it into the bottom of the metal bucket and wadded up some newspapers and threw them in on top. She doused it with a little bit of the lighter fluid and then she took the book of matches out of her pocket.

It took her several tries to light the match and then it went out in the breeze that was blowing through the alley. She tried again, this time much closer to the newspaper wads and managed to light the newspapers on fire. The lighter fluid made the fire burst up quickly and Mona had to jump backwards to avoid the flames.

She watched as the newspapers burned down rapidly and the flames crept towards the plant at the bottom.

Suddenly, a shrill scream filled the air. Mona had to cover her ears with her hands. She dropped to her knees from the sound. Mona managed to look up and saw the plant trying to crawl out of the bucket. It was on fire and was using its roots as hands to try to climb out.

Mona staggered over to the lighter fluid and grabbed the yellow bottle. She aimed it at the plant and squirted more fluid at the plant.

The plant shrieked shrilly again and fell back into the bucket as the flames shot skyward.

The shrieking grew silent and Mona was able to stand up again. She stared into the bucket and looked at the plant. The fire was starting to burn down, and the plant's remains slightly resembled a tiny creature of some sort. Not a plant, but something more animal-like. The fire continued to burn it until it collapsed completely into ash at the bottom of the bucket. The fire extinguished itself and left Mona staring into a now empty bucket.

After Mona cleaned up any evidence of her having a tiny bonfire in the back alley, including returning the still warm bucket and the lighter fluid to the basement, she went back upstairs to her computer.

She sent a message to PlantMan662, "I did it. I burned it. It was a creature of some sort."

A few minutes later, PlantMan662 replied, "Good. Now don't go back to see your sister. Ever."

Mona sighed. How would she explain that? Not wanting to see her sister after instigating a visit and even taking a plant cutting? Suddenly not wanting anything to do with Silvia seemed awfully callous.

Mona wondered if those golden eyes really meant Silvia was a fae.

She decided she would go over to see Silvia one last time.

This time, she had a plan.

* 6 *

Mona spent the day researching on the internet. Halfway through the day, she realized that she had completely forgotten to go to school. After a few moments of panic, she decided that she would deal with the consequences when they came. For right now, she had more research to do.

Mona was now ready to believe that fae were real, and that her sister was a changeling. There was no other explanation for what she had witnessed when she burned the plant. Her sister was definitely fae. Mona had no idea what that meant for her father and his new soon-to-be wife.

When three o'clock rolled around, Mona was ready to make one more visit to see her sister.

She packed up a thermos she had filled with a special tea and a piece of wrought iron from a broken balcony rail she had found in the basement and put them in her backpack.

Mona took a deep breath and headed to see her sister.

Moments after she knocked on the front door, Silvia answered by swinging the door open with a happy squeal.

"You came back!" Silvia said happily as she embraced Mona.

Mona hugged her back, not wanting to give away the real intention of her visit.

Once inside the red living room again, Silvia offered Mona a snack.

"Sure, whatever," Mona agreed. Although she had no intention of eating or drinking anything her sister had to offer.

During her research, she had discovered that eating or drinking anything offered by a fae would make you theirs forever. Mona didn't plan to go that route.

Silvia came over with some cookies and milk and they sat down at a little table near a window in the kitchen.

The sunlight poured in through the window and made Silvia's golden hair and eyes glimmer in an eerie way.

Mona was becoming more and more sure that her sister was indeed, a changeling.

When Silvia went to pour Mona some milk, Mona stopped her.

"Actually, I brought some tea with me," Mona said. "I feel like I've been fighting off a cold. Do you happen to have a mug I could use?"

"Sure," Silvia went quickly to the kitchen and retrieved a red mug for Mona to use. "Here."

Mona took the mug from Silvia and pulled the thermos out of her backpack.

"It's my own special brew," Mona said. "Anytime I feel the slightest tickle of a cold, I make this. I never get sick."

She poured some of the tea into her mug.

Silvia leaned over the table and looked at the tea, "What's it taste like?"

"It's actually good," Mona said. "I put in licorice to make it taste sweet. And it's good for a sore throat."

"Can I taste it?" Silvia asked.

Mona smiled and slid the mug towards her sister. This was exactly what she was hoping for. "Sure, go ahead."

She watched as Silvia took a sip and made a face and shoved it back towards Mona, "Eew that's really gross. What else is in it?"

"Oh, some chamomile, ground up eggshells," Mona started.

"Ground up eggshells?" Silvia made another face. "Gross."

"It works," Mona said. She made a mmmm noise as she took a sip and tried not to make the same face that her sister did. "It's good.

"I'll stick with milk,'" Silvia said.

Just then, Silvia's mother came in the front door with their father.

"Hi, Dad," Mona said. The disappointment in her voice was more because her plan was now ruined, but she could see the hurt look on his face at the unenthusiastic greeting.

"Daddy!" Silvia squealed and ran into his arms for a big hug.

Silvia's mother came over and smiled at Mona.

"Hello, you must be Ramona," she said. "My name is Ella."

Mona nodded, "I know."

Ella sat down in Silvia's place across the table from Mona.

"I know a lot has happened, but I am hoping we can become friends," Ella said.

Mona shrugged. She was wondering if one sip was enough for the tea to work on Silvia, and if it was, how long such a small amount would last.

"What is this?" Ella gestured at the mug of tea. "It smells wonderful."

"Mona brought tea," Silvia skipped to the table, holding her father's hand and bringing him with her.

"May I try it?" Ella asked. "I just love licorice."

Mona shrugged.

Ella took a large sip and then slammed the mug down onto the table.

"How dare you come into this house with that?" Ella stood and leaned over the kitchen table and glared down at Mona.

"Ella, what?" Mona's father reached towards Ella.

Ella flipped the table across the small kitchen to clear the path between her and Mona.

"She put ground eggshells in the tea," Ella said.

Mona's father tried to step in front of Mona, who was frozen in place in her chair, "I don't understand."

"Move out of the way Micah," Ella shoved Mona's father to the floor with no effort. He slid into the refrigerator and bumped his head against it with a loud thud.

"Ground eggshells in tea make a changeling admit who she is," Ella said. "You thought it was Silvia? You were so wrong, child. The changeling is me."

"Run," Micah yelled from the kitchen floor. "Mona, run."

Mona scrambled away from the chair she was still sitting in and tried to make it across the red living room to the front door. She tripped over her open backpack and tried to get back to her feet.

Ella was right behind her and grabbed her by the hair.

Mona yelped in pain as the changeling started to change to her true form and pulled Mona by the hair to face her. Ella's mouth had grown in size and she had three rows of teeth. Her eyes were like a snake's and she had scales where her ears should be.

"Mom," Silvia was in tears. "What's happening?"

Mona managed to look over at Silvia, who looked honestly horrified at the sight of her mother.

"That's right," Ella hissed. "Silvia is only a half-breed. She's not the one you had to worry about."

Ella drew back her free hand, which now had elongated fingers and talon-like nails. As she went to swipe at Mona, she suddenly let out a hissing squeal and released her grip.

Mona dropped to the red shag carpet with a painful thud. She scrambled to get out of the way as Ella collapsed to the floor.

Mona's father was standing behind Ella, breathing heavily. The piece of wrought iron from Mona's backpack was sticking out of Ella's back. Her body steamed like it was cooking and then slowly disappeared.

"I'm so sorry, Mona," her father looked down at her. "She had me enthralled."

"What?" Mona looked around for Silvia.

The girl was slumped over on the floor, still near the kitchen table.

Mona crawled over to her sister, suddenly feeling sorry for her.

"What's happening?" Mona's father asked.

"When a mother changeling dies, so do all of her children," Mona whispered.

Silvia looked up at Mona with her golden eyes, "I really would've liked to have been your sister."

Mona's eyes welled with tears as she took hold of her little sister. As she did, the girl went up in a steaming billow, just like her mother. Mona was left with tears streaming down her face and empty arms.

Mona's father was already at her side. "She didn't know. She never knew."

"She didn't know she was half-fae?" Mona looked at her father.

For the first time in a long time, Mona felt like she actually recognized her father.

He shook his head, "No. She was a half-breed, so she had no real power. Ella never told her."

"Is Ella why you," Mona choked on her words.

Her father nodded, "I met her one day when I was out for a jog. She offered me some water. It was a hot day, and I was parched. And the water looked so refreshing."

"You drank something offered by a fairy," Mona said.

"I couldn't help it," her father said through tears of his own. "It just looked so good."

"It's okay," Mona whispered.

Mona hugged her father for the first time in almost a year. "Everything's okay."

THE BUTTERFLY BOY

Icarus always thought he had an unfortunate name. His mother loved mythology and named each of her children, and pets, after her favorite mythological characters.

After four brothers, two sisters, six dogs, three cats, a bird, a lizard, sixteen goldfish, and a turtle, his mother was running low on the good names. So, Icarus it was.

He wouldn't have minded it so badly, except for the fact that the kids at school called him Icky, among other things. So did his brothers for that matter. His sisters did as well, but only when they were angry with him.

He also didn't like the fact that his name wasn't borrowed from a hero, but from someone to not be like. Many times, Icarus pictured his namesake falling from the sky after disobeying his father and flying too close to the sun. He was named after someone who was doomed.

Unlike his namesake, Icarus kept to the shadows. He wanted to hide from the ones who called him Icky. Icarus preferred not to be seen.

When the other children were playing on the playground, Icarus would find a place far away from the other children. He usually either quietly read, or he laid on his back with his arms behind his head and watched the clouds move across the sky.

Icarus wasn't sure exactly when the butterflies first started coming.

The first one came by itself, so did the second, and the third, and so on. They were just part of the scenery. Part of the peace that came from being alone. Sometimes he noticed them, sometimes he didn't. It was when they came in a small swarm that Icarus finally really took notice.

He was laying in the grass one day, at the farthest end of the soccer field. He found that he was usually safe out behind the farthest goal net. The bullies who called him Icky didn't like to walk out that far just to get their kicks. They settled on kids that stayed closer to the playground. Just like animals in the wild, they stalked the easier prey.

Icarus could hear them in the distance. It was Eugene's turn today. A boy with another unfortunate name. Icarus felt bad for Eugene, but he tried to block out the badness of the world when he was out this far.

Icarus felt the blades of grass tickle his arms and his ears. He shifted around a little bit until he became more comfortable. The smell of freshly cut grass was sharp to his nose and he decided he liked the strong smell, even though he felt like the cuttings were stuck in his throat. The grass was also slightly damp from the early morning sprinklers, but in the moment he didn't care.

Icarus stared up at the sky and made a game out of naming what each cloud looked like. He saw a tiger, a giraffe, and a Volkswagen bug move slowly and gracefully across his view.

While he was trying to decide if a certain cloud looked more like a horse or a train, he saw a swarm of butterflies flit above him. It was the fact that there were so many of them that caught his attention. He had never seen so many at once. He rolled over in the grass as they flew past and across the field, so that he could keep them in view.

They were the most beautiful thing he had ever seen. The orange and black of their wings flitting wildly against the blue sky. They seemed so graceful and chaotic as they flew across the field and flitted up the hill and disappeared over the high wall that led to one of the houses in the neighborhood that bordered the school.

Once they were out of sight, Icarus felt happy. He felt like he just saw something wondrous. Something that was meant just for him and was all his own. Something he didn't have to share with classmates or siblings. The butterflies came for him.

He heard the bell off in the distance that signified that recess was over. He sat up and went to gather up his book and his jacket. Icarus looked down at his shorts and suddenly realized with a shock that laying on freshly cut wet grass might not have been the best idea.

The back of his shorts were covered in green stains. He reached around and pulled his shirt by the shoulder to try to get a look at the back of his shirt, but he couldn't see it. So, he pulled his arms into his sleeves and spun his shirt around. He looked down to see that the back of his light-yellow shirt was completely stained with grass green blotches.

Icarus sighed and turned his shirt back around. He pulled on his jacket, over the grass stains, and tried to pull it down as far as he could over the back of his shorts. It wouldn't reach far enough, so deciding shirt stains were better than stains on the back of his shorts, he pulled off his jacket and tied it around his waist.

He picked up his book and started to jog back across the soccer field and back to class. He realized that he was going to be late if he didn't hurry. And the last thing he wanted was to have all eyes on him when he walked into the classroom late, and covered with wet green stains.

Icarus suffered through the rest of the day. The laughing, the jeers, the other students calling him Icky Sticky. The bullies were waiting to taunt him and push him down into the grass out in front of the school so that he would have matching grass stains on the front of his clothes. The day went past in a blur to Icarus.

What got him through were the butterflies.

They were all he could think about. As he lay on the grass face down, with the foot of one of the bullies grinding down in the center of his back, his mind went blank, except for the butterflies. He was out on the field again, watching the swarm flit across the blue background of the spring sky. They danced around him and showed off their majestic orange markings. Even after the bullies left to go home, Icarus stayed on the ground and imagined the but-terflies coming again just for him.

Once at home, the butterflies were all he could think about. He spent the evening researching butterflies. He ignored his home-work and studied everything he could find about them.

The next day, Icarus came prepared. He had put a small picnic blanket in his backpack. His mother kept it in the hall closet, way in the back. He had to stand on the bottom shelf to reach it, push-ing all of the old towels and rags out of the way to dig back into the very back where he remembered it being hidden.

It was perfect. Red and white checkered pattern on the top, a plastic protective layer sewn to the bottom. It was smashed oddly from being in the back of the linen closet. But Icarus smuggled it into the basement, where he had a small reading corner all to him-self. His siblings didn't like the basement, so they left him alone when he was down there. He knew he was safe to spread out the blanket, smooth it out the best he could, and then refold it as neatly as a plastic blanket would fold to fit into his backpack with all of his books and supplies.

The bullies couldn't bother him that morning. At least he thought they couldn't.

But they were merciless. The cool spring morning had covered the grass with a coating of dew, and the gardeners still hadn't adjusted the sprinklers out on the field. As Icarus headed out towards the soccer field at recess, the bullies stopped him just before he could set foot on the grass.

Icarus stood on the graying asphalt, looking down at the ground where the cracked and crumbling asphalt gave way to the muddy edge of the grassy field.

He tuned out their insults and jeers, and when he gave them no reaction, they shoved him down into the mud.

Icarus landed with a splash and he felt the cold slimy mud squish through his fingers. His arms weren't ready for the impact, so his chest splashed down into the cold wet muddy puddle, drenching his shirt to his skin. The grit of the mud crunched between his teeth as he tried to spit his mouth clear.

The other boys laughed and left him there to pull himself out of the mud. His shirt was darkened and his bare arms were coated with muck.

He crawled over to the grass and stood up on sturdier ground. He held his arms away from himself and looked at his mud-covered clothes.

Icarus watched as the bullies walked away, guffawing and slapping each other on the back, occasionally turning to point and laugh at Icarus. He stood there, dripping with mud in the sunshine, spitting a seemingly endless supply of mud and grit into the grass.

Icarus wanted nothing more than to go home, change his clothes, and crawl back under the covers and go back to sleep. He wanted to pretend this day had never happened. He wanted to be dry. He didn't want to go back to his classroom covered in mud. In fact, he didn't want to go back at all. The title of Icky Sticky would cement itself to Icarus when he went back. Something he didn't feel he could ever live down. Too many of his other classmates had caught on to it the day before.

But then he remembered his goal. The butterflies.

Icarus pulled out a towel he had packed in his backpack with his picnic blanket. He had thought to pack it just in case. He wished that he had thought to pack an extra shirt. He was able to use the towel to wipe the mud off of his face and most of it from his arms, but by that time it was too damp and muddy to even attempt to fix his shirt.

Icarus left the towel on the ground at the edge of the mud puddle, picked up his backpack, and headed to the far end of the soccer field. When he got there, he spread out his picnic blanket on the ground behind the soccer net.

He looked at his arms, which were still streaked with mud, and sighed. He laid down on his red and white checked picnic blanket and stared up at the sky. The clouds were fewer and farther between that day. And the wind didn't blow them across the sky. They sat high up in the air, like big cotton balls spilled from a bag.

His muddy shirt stuck to his chest; a cold layer of wet filth pressed against him that reminded him of why he hid out in the depths of the soccer field.

He shut his eyes, just for a moment, to soak in the warmth of the sun. He wanted to forget the chill of the mud and the shrieking laughter of the bullies. The warmth of the sun felt good. He could feel the mud drying and the world slipping away.

When he opened his eyes, they were there. The butterflies hovered above him, flitting gracefully and wildly against the blue sky and white cotton that hung above them.

He lifted his arm and held his hand out to the butterflies. One of them flitted towards him and landed on his outstretched hand. He brought it closer to his face and watched as the beautiful orange and black winged creature slowly opened and closed its wings as it perched on his index finger. Icarus could see the delicate pattern of the bright orange dots on the creature's wings.

He wished he could be part of their orange and black kaleidoscope, flitting about in the spring sunshine.

Icarus laid back on his blanket and stared up at the other butterflies. They stayed close, not wanting to leave their friend. Icarus held his hand gently and let the butterfly sit on his finger for as long as it liked.

It was peaceful. Icarus wished he could stay like that forever. Laying on the grass, with a butterfly perched on his finger. Watching the kaleidoscope of the other butterflies flitting happily above him against the dappled white and vivid blue sky.

Icarus could hear shouts off in the distance. He tore his eyes away from the butterflies and saw that the bullies were heading across the field towards him.

He started to panic. The last thing he wanted was for the bullies to invade his safe place and see the butterflies. They weren't something he was ready to share with anyone, especially not them.

"You have to fly away now," he told the butterfly that was nestled on his finger.

It answered him by slowly flapping its wings.

The other butterflies came down from the sky. They swarmed around Icarus and each took a place at the edge of his red and white checked picnic blanket.

The butterflies lifted the edges of the blanket and Icarus could feel himself rising up off the ground. He laid back in the blanket to balance himself and let the butterflies lift him up, high above the soccer field.

Icarus could hear the bullies shouting below him, but they couldn't reach him.

The butterflies carried Icarus high into the sky. He kept his eyes on the butterflies flitting wildly against the blue sky as they carried him off to where the butterflies go. Somewhere safe from the bullies. Somewhere where it was acceptable to be covered in mud.

The butterflies flew high, but they kept Icarus from flying too close to the sun. And Icarus knew that the kaleidoscope of tiny little wings would never let him fall.

THE REPLACEMENT

NO ONE ASKED WHAT HAPPENED to the butterfly boy. The child who was whisked away by a kaleidoscope of Monarch butterflies one day during recess. He had brought a red and white checked picnic blanket to school with him, to protect himself from the cold mud and wet grass as he laid on the ground at the farthest end of the soccer field and watched the clouds drift by.

The butterflies came in a swarm of dancing orange and black and carried him off to protect him from the bullies that were coming for him. To do him harm.

There were a few whispers here and there about what may have been seen that day, but no one dared to speak of it out loud. To say that you witnessed a child being kidnapped by a kaleidoscope of butterflies would make you an object of ridicule, wouldn't it?

Especially since his mother didn't even notice he was gone.

But that was only because the changeling child replaced him so seamlessly.

He looked just like the butterfly boy, an exact duplicate in every way. The only difference was a birthmark on his shoulder. Some said it actually looked like a butterfly.

But the changeling boy was different.

He didn't let the bullies get away with beating him up. He was strong. When one of the bullies tried to shove him down into the mud, the changeling boy turned the tables on the bully. And for the first time, the bully tasted the mud that he shoved so many other children down into. He didn't even know how he got there, his mouth full of muck and grit. But when the changeling boy was finished with him, that bully didn't feel like bullying other children anymore.

Eventually, the changeling boy grew up. He never fit in with his peers. He stayed in the shadows, away from everyone else. But he always acted as a guardian to the ones who were bullied.

I watched him from the secret corners and dark shadows that allowed me a view into his world. He was always an oddity, but he lived my life better than I ever did. Of course, I was a child when he took my place. Still in elementary school. I never had much of a chance to live.

It was years before I knew a changeling had taken my place. I was raised by the butterflies that had absconded with me. And the fairies that lived with them. They had been my family for years. I was happy. But the fairies had me under a spell.

It wasn't until there was an accident in the forest one night that the spell was broken. There had been a terrible thunderstorm, and the fairy that had cast my spell was hit by lightning. She was killed instantly, and just as fast, the spell that had me in their thrall was broken.

The shock of realizing how many years I had lost came slowly. Especially since I didn't even know what year it was, or how old I was for that matter. Fairies didn't usually keep track of things that way.

All I knew was that I needed to find my family. I had been gone for years; I thought my mother would be devastated. Imagine my surprise when I went to my childhood home and not only was my family still there, but so was I.

I had heard of changelings from the whispers among the butterflies. But they didn't like to answer my questions about them and while under the fairy's spell, they could change the subject without much argument from me.

I watched the changeling with my family through the window each night. They had no idea he wasn't really me. Most of my older brothers and sisters had moved out. He, I was around sixteen, and was the youngest of seven. So, my family had gotten much smaller. Just my mother, the changeling, and two of my older brothers sat down to dinner each night. The rest, presumably, were in college or out on their own by then.

It broke my heart and spurred on my anger as I realized how much I had lost. I didn't even know where to find my other siblings.

I had to make things right. I had to take my life back.

One night, I went out into the tool shed and found an old pair of pruning shears. They were very old and a bit rusty, but still sharp.

I went back out to the back window where I had been watching my family have dinner with the imposter. They were inside, cleaning up. The changeling was at the sink washing dishes while my mother was still clearing the table. My brothers were busying themselves with not helping, making me realize that some things never change.

I stood just outside the window, in the shadows. I didn't want my mother to see. But I did want him to see.

The changeling boy looked up and he did see me. Our eyes locked and I motioned for him to come outside.

He said something to my mother and dried his hands. He went to the back door. I waited for him just outside. I stayed hidden and ready.

I caught him off guard. It was easier to kill him than I thought it would be. And just when I was trying to decide what to do with the body, he faded away and disappeared. Like he never was.

I waited for my mother to go upstairs, and then I snuck inside. I cleaned up and changed into some fresh clothing, the first I'd had in years.

I knew I wouldn't fit in at first, with all the time I had lost. I never had fit in. I never had the chance.

But now, finally, I had the chance to try. I had stolen back my life. The butterfly boy was home.

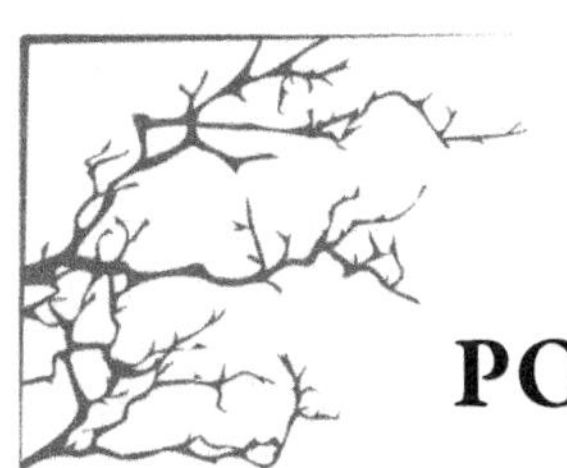

POOKA DEALS

Sometimes Quinn Albright hated her job. When she had decided to become a PI, she thought it would be fun, maybe even exciting.

Instead, she wound up working for an investment company to pay the bills. Her job was to perform due diligence before the company invested in anything new. It was her job to make sure that there was no fraud being committed and that the investment wasn't some sort of a Ponzi scheme.

She was a paper pusher.

And she hated it.

But not tonight.

Tonight, her most recent case led her to a Mr. Noah Larson.

The problem was, he was supposed to be dead.

But here she was, out in the middle of the night, trailing Mr. Larson to the edge of town.

He had left a lot of money to the company she worked for when he died.

She had first heard about it through the rumor mill, but thought nothing of it until her boss called her into his office and asked her to find Mr. Larson.

"I'm sorry," she said. "Isn't he the guy that died?"

She was sitting in Mr. Nguyen's office. He had the best office on the floor, as far as Quinn was concerned. It was a corner office, with a view of the city out not one wall, but two. One side even had a view that overlooked the river.

Mr. Nguyen had his desk strategically placed so that he could see the river and his door from where he sat. But Quinn, in the chair in front of his desk, could see neither.

She didn't have to go in there very often. But when she did, it made her very nervous. Mr. Nguyen never saw anyone unless it was something major. And he usually fired people who did unsatisfactory work.

"Yes, he is the man who left us a lot of money in a trust. He requested that we consider distributing the money to various charitable organizations," Mr. Nguyen said. "But we suspect he's still alive. And if he is, we don't want to accept any of this money. It could lead to lawsuits that we don't care to deal with. I want you to make sure that he is dead. And if he's not, find out what he's up to and why he wanted us to take his money."

"Is there a reason that he chose this company to be his executor?" Quinn asked.

"If you happen to find him, maybe you can ask him that too," Mr. Nguyen said. "He has no connection to the company that we know of, no reason that we can see that he would choose us to make those financial decisions for him. Especially since he has family. Distant kin, but still family according to the law."

He handed Quinn the file. She flipped through it and looked up at her boss.

"I know this is unusual," Mr. Nguyen said. "But you're our top investigator. Your recommendations have been on the mark every single time. So, I'm confident you can do this."

Quinn thanked Mr. Nguyen, took the folder, and left his office.

She flipped through the file as she walked down the beige hallway and back to her office. With her single window that had a view of the building across the way.

Quinn racked her brain as she tried to think of where to start looking for a dead man.

She sat down in front of the laptop she kept in her office and brought up all the information she could find on Mr. Larson.

He led a fairly normal life. He worked at an investment firm, not unlike her own. He had been an associate, well on his way up the corporate ladder when he suddenly retired early last year.

He had no wife, no children, his parents had passed away years ago. The only family he had were cousins that he didn't really seem to have anything to do with.

Quinn checked his social media pages online. He only had professional links and very little was posted that wasn't about his professional life. His social media activity ended when he retired. There was no other sign of him online.

She checked his credit history and criminal record. He was clean. Boring. Just an average guy who focused his entire life on his work because he really didn't have much else.

Quinn stared at the screen wondering what it was that had made him retire early.

She looked at his credit history. The last major purchase he had made on his credit card was a trip to the Caribbean. Which he had fully paid off, she noted. He retired shortly after his trip.

She also noticed in the file that his funeral was the following day. She figured that was as good of a place to start as any and planned to attend.

She figured, who would want to miss their own funeral?

THE FOLLOWING DAY, Quinn dressed in black. She made sure she was wearing low heeled shoes because it was going to be a graveside service. She didn't want to spend the afternoon pulling her heels out of the grass.

She hovered near the back, so she could watch things clearly. She was curious to see who would show up. This man had no close family, and hadn't worked in over a year.

She was right when she figured it would be a very low turnout. And of the few who came, not one shed a tear for the man.

It was a closed casket, so she had no idea if he was really in the casket that was being lowered into the ground, and she couldn't think of a good reason to ask the mortuary if they would open it for her before the ceremony.

She was getting ready to leave when she noticed a dark shadow off to her left. She turned to look and saw a man skulking around behind a tree, watching the memorial service from a distance.

The man matched Mr. Larson's approximate weight and height.

Quinn needed to get a closer look to be sure.

She tilted her head away from the man and headed back to her car, hoping he wouldn't take notice of her as the casket was being lowered into the ground.

Quinn circled back from the parking area and tried to get a better look at the man.

As far as she could tell, he was Noah Larson. He looked just like the pictures she had seen of him online.

He put on a pair of sunglasses and pulled his hat lower down over his face and headed to his car.

Quinn raced back to her car, determined to follow him.

She tried to remember everything she had learned about how to tail someone. It had been a long since she had last done it. She was sure she was following too close, in hopes of not losing his vehicle in traffic.

He got onto the highway and headed south.

She knew she could follow him at a much larger distance on the highway, but she wondered where he was headed.

She was sure this was the right guy.

Quinn started getting nervous as his car headed across the state line. She called into work and left a message for Mr. Nguyen that she was fairly sure that she had found Mr. Larson and was currently following his vehicle south on the interstate.

Her assistant checked the license plate number for her and verified that it was a rental.

"Be careful," her assistant had said before hanging up. "I have a bad feeling that this guy doesn't want to be found for a reason."

"Then he shouldn't have gone to his own funeral," Quinn said.

They drove for hours, only stopping occasionally for gas. Quinn tried to stop at alternate gas stations or park at opposite ends of the lot when they stopped.

At one rest stop, he had left while she was still in the bathroom, and it was several miles of panicking and driving over the speed limit before she caught up to him again.

She wondered if he had noticed her following him at this point. They had been driving the same route, making the same stops all day.

She kept up the ruse and was glad that she had thought to bring more comfortable clothes with her to change out of after the funeral. But she had yet to do so.

They drove into the night, and Quinn hoped and prayed that she would stay awake while driving. It had been a long day and they had travelled through several states. It was much harder to follow someone in the dark. She only hoped that she was still following the right set of tail lights in the darkness.

When they finally crossed the state line into Louisiana, Quinn was fairly sure they were headed to New Orleans. What she didn't know was why.

She wondered if there was some connection to his trip to the Caribbean that changed the direction of his life and now brought him here to New Orleans.

Quinn followed Larson to the French Quarter, where he parked his car and set out on foot. She parked her car, and was glad that she hadn't had time to change out of her funeral outfit, with the exception of her shoes, and set out on foot after him.

She followed him for quite a way. He never looked behind him to see if he was being followed. He seemed to be walking with a singular focus.

He walked off the main well-lit street and down a darker side street. It was much sleepier than the main-street where a few establishments were still open and tourists enjoyed the late-night life.

But as they went deeper down the unlit side street, it got quieter and much more ominous in the darkness.

She quietly crept along behind him, fairly sure that he had no idea she was still there.

He went around a corner and into an alley between two dark buildings. When Quinn got there, she could see two doors in the alley, and a wall at the end with no other exit. Mr. Larson was gone.

She stood between the two doors, looking back and forth between them. Quinn figured she had a fifty-fifty chance of picking the right door, so she chose the blue one.

It was locked.

She turned and looked at the green one, took a deep breath and tried the knob.

It was locked as well.

"Crap," she muttered to herself.

She still didn't know which door to pick.

But it didn't matter, because Mr. Larson came out of the shadows and slammed her up against the brick wall beside the green door. He held his arm against her throat so tightly that it lifted her a few inches, leaving her scrambling to keep her toes on the ground.

"Why are you following me?" he demanded.

"Mr. Larson?" she hoped using his name would calm him down, but it only seemed to make him angrier.

"Who sent you?" he demanded, slamming her against the wall even harder.

Cornered and being threatened in a dark alley, Quinn decided that the truth was her best course of action.

"My boss," Quinn said, gasping for breath. "Mr. Nguyen, he didn't believe you were dead."

Larson almost laughed; he loosened his hold against her slightly. "This is about the money?"

Quin just nodded as best as she could, too scared to find any more words.

Larson released her completely and she lowered herself back down onto her feet.

Every part of her being wanted to send a knee hard into his groin, but since she needed answers, she held herself in check.

"You can tell your boss that the money is his, free and clear," Larson laughed again. "Where I'm going, I will have no need for money."

"Where are you going?" she asked, rubbing her throat with one hand.

"I can't tell you," he said. "But as far as this world is concerned, I'm as good as dead."

"What do you mean?' she asked.

Larson started walking back up the alley towards the street.

"Stop following me," he said over his shoulder.

Quinn had to almost jog to keep up with him.

"I can't go back until I have some answers," she said. "My boss will never take the money if he knows that you're alive."

"Then don't tell him," Larson said. "I need him to take that money."

"Why?" Quinn was thoroughly confused. "Where is it that you are going?"

A large man stepped out from another alleyway as they were making their way down the street.

"I told you to come alone," the man said.

Quinn stopped next to Mr. Larson and stood staring up at the huge man.

He stood well over six and a half feet tall and he was enormous. He was solidly built, all muscle. She tried in vain to see his face in the darkness, but under the fedora hat he was wearing, it seemed like shadow was always over his face.

"Did you do as you were told?" the man asked.

"Every bit of it," Larson said.

"Then why do you have an escort?" the man asked, nodding at Quinn.

Larson just sighed and looked at Quinn.

"She's nobody," Larson said. "She can go back and tell her boss she followed the wrong person, and that I really am dead."

The huge man shook his head no. "She knows," he said. "You failed."

"No, please," Larson begged. "I did everything you asked."

"You failed," the man said. "Unless she is willing to come with us."

Larson looked back at Quinn, "She'll come. She wants answers."

"You bet I want answers," Quinn said. "And I'm not leaving until I have them."

"You heard her," Larson said eagerly. "She said she'll come. Voluntarily."

The man just let out a chuckle and then turned on his heel and led them down another dark alleyway.

Quinn started wondering if this was a good idea.

It was too late to turn back, she thought. She was all in.

They reached a building that had a large set of double doors. It seemed out of place, from what Quinn could tell. She had no idea what would be waiting for her on the other side of those doors.

The man turned and looked at Quinn.

"You can't bring your phone," he said to her.

"What?" Quinn was really thinking this was all a very bad idea. She considered just turning back. Reporting what she had seen so far, and letting Mr. Nguyen decide what to do about the rest.

She knew Larson was alive.

But she still didn't know what he was up to, and that was part of her assignment.

Quinn looked around and then up at the man.

"What do you want me to do with it?" she asked.

He just put out a gloved hand.

Quinn pulled her cell phone from her pocket and held it in her hand for a moment.

Without her cell phone, she had no way to call for help. And the last time she had texted her assistant was back at the car.

No one would know where to find her.

She handed the man her phone.

He immediately dropped it on the ground and smashed it with one of his huge feet.

"Hey," she said. "Why did you have to do that?"

"No technology," he said.

She was suddenly glad she had left her purse in the car. Her extra laptop and personal phone were still safe in there.

"You can't just walk in here," the man said.

"What do you mean?" Quinn looked back and forth between the two men.

"Get ready for the ride of your life," Larson laughed. He hopped up and down and rubbed his hands together like a small child ready for a reward.

Quin would've thought he was crazy if her attention hadn't been drawn to the huge man standing in front of her. He bent forward and his arms grew long and changed shape. His body morphed in the darkness and he became a large black stallion, stamping at the ground in front of her.

"Now we ride!" Larson gleefully jumped up onto the horse's back.

He reached a hand down to Quinn. Still in shock, she absently reached up to Larson's hand that was extended down to her and he pulled her up. She allowed herself to be whisked up onto the horse so that she was sitting behind him on the horse's back.

"Hold on," Larson hollered.

The horse kicked open the double doors and Quinn was suddenly blinded by a bright light that appeared in the doorway. She involuntarily threw her arms around Mr. Larson's waist in a desperate attempt to not get bucked off and left behind.

The horse leapt straight into the light and the next thing Quinn knew, they were flying on horseback over a grassy terrain.

It was daylight and she could see clearly as they flew through the clouds and then angled down towards the ground at a frightening speed.

When they landed, she and Larson climbed off the horse together and stood looking around.

"Where are we?" she asked.

"Does it matter?" Larson asked. "Look at this place!"

Larson wandered off into the grassy field and behaved like he clearly saw something that Quinn did not.

The horse shifted again beside her and the familiar deep voice asked her, "What do you see?"

"Nothing," she shook her head. "Just Larson in an empty grass field."

She turned and looked at the man/horse, who was now a large rabbit looking down at her.

"What the heck?" she took a step backwards. "What are you?"

"I'm a pooka," he said proudly. "Look out at the field again."

"A what?" she asked.

"Look again," he pointed past her to the field.

When Quinn looked back, she was faced with the most beautiful garden she had ever seen. There was a tiered fountain in the center and the base was surrounded by beds of pansies.

A grass pathway went in a circle around it with pathways leading to large and beautiful beds of some of Quinn's favorite spring flowers. There was every color Quinn could imagine.

Sitting on the edge of the fountain was the most beautiful woman she had ever seen. She had long blonde hair that flowed down her back. She wore a green dress that was tied with a golden cord around her waist. She turned and saw Quinn looking at her, and she stood up from the edge of the fountain and started coming towards her.

"Welcome," the woman said. "My name is Aurora; you must be Quinn."

"How did you know my name?" Quinn asked.

As the woman got closer, Quinn noticed that the woman had pointed ears sticking out through her hair.

"I know the name of everyone who comes to my garden," Aurora said.

Quinn looked back at the pooka, but he was gone. So was Larson.

"Where did they go?" Quinn asked.

"Who?" Aurora asked.

Quinn looked back over her shoulder again. The garden continued on behind her, with its colorful flowers stretching as far as the eye could see. Butterflies flitted around everywhere, making the garden feel even more magical than it looked.

"I don't know," Quinn shook her head. "I thought-"

"I have something to show you," Aurora said.

She took Quinn by the hand and led her back to the fountain.

Quinn followed Aurora over to the water and looked into the fountain where Aurora was pointing.

She saw her own reflection in the water. She now wore a flower crown on her head and a golden dress that matched the one Aurora wore. Hers was tied with a green cord around the waist.

"What would you like to do today?" Aurora asked.

Quinn, completely unable to tear her eyes away from her own reflection, felt like she had come here for a reason. She just couldn't think of why.

"I don't know," Quinn said. "What would you like to do?"

Aurora smiled and said, "Follow me."

Aurora took Quinn by the hand and took off running. Quinn followed closely behind her, enjoying the feel of the warm breeze on her face as they went. They ran into a beautiful forest and Aurora showed Quinn the magic of the trees.

Quinn felt like she had never been so happy in all her life. She watched pixies playing in the forest and she and Aurora played hide and seek with them. She felt as if all of her worries and cares had melted off of her and she felt completely free.

As the sun was setting, Aurora led Quinn back to the fountain and there the pooka was waiting for her in his black stallion disguise.

"Come with me," he said.

"Where are we going?" Quinn asked.

"Climb on," he ordered.

"You'd better go," Aurora said. "But come back to see me soon, I had such fun today."

Aurora hugged Quinn goodbye and Quinn climbed up onto the horse's back.

The ride back was like a bucket of cold water being thrown on her and she remembered why she had come.

But by the time she remembered that she was supposed to be looking for what happened to Mr. Larson, the pooka was already standing with her on the dark street as the double doors slammed shut behind them.

"Wait," she said. "I need to go back."

Quinn threw herself against the doors, but they were locked up tight.

"If you're worried about Mr. Larson," the pooka said. "You no longer need to. He will never return to this world. You can tell your boss that you followed the wrong man and that Mr. Larson is dead and buried."

"I don't care about Mr. Larson," she said, pounding on the door desperately. "I just need to go back."

The pooka smiled.

"There are some conditions," he said.

"What are they?" she asked. She turned and looked at him with wild-eyed torment.

"You must sever all ties with this world," the pooka said. "You must rid yourself of all money, but you cannot spend it nor can you give it away to someone who needs it or will use it."

"What?" she asked. "Why?"

"These are the conditions," he said. "You must fake your death. No one must come looking for you. That is where Mr. Larson failed us."

"What happens if I fail?" she asked.

"Then you cannot enter back into our world," he said.

"But you let Larson back in," she said.

The pooka just laughed. "Did we?"

"Didn't you?" she asked.

"And finally," the pooka stared down at her. "You will never return to this world. You will stay with us forever."

"Okay," she said. "Fine, whatever."

"You may return to us when these things are done," the pooka said.

"Okay," she said. "I'll be back."

Quinn ran to her car.

She breathlessly texted her assistant that it was the wrong man, and that she was on her way home.

The whole drive back to the city, Quinn had a heady feeling that made everything feel like a dream. She couldn't stop thinking about Aurora's world and getting back to it. She longed for the feeling of freedom and happiness that she experienced while she was there.

When she got home, she set out to create a trust to take care of her money and other assets. She set it up the same way Mr. Larson had, leaving the money to a large business with the recommendation that they give it all to charity on their own behalf.

Then she set out to fake her own death.

In her hurry, she decided that the best way was to push her car into the river. Hopefully the authorities would find it, and assume she had drowned, and declare her dead after she had been missing for a while.

She then bought a bus ticket with a small stash of cash she had set aside for the trip, and headed back to New Orleans.

It was a long bus ride. When she finally got there, she waited for the pooka in front of the double doors, anxious to get back to the garden.

Late that night, he finally showed up.

"You had a lot of people looking for you," he said.

"What?" she didn't understand.

"You failed the test when you had people searching for your body," he said. "People are still looking for you."

"But they will declare me dead soon and no one will ever find me anyway," Quinn said desperately. "Just take me back."

The pooka smiled and opened the doors. He turned into the black stallion so she could climb up onto his back and they flew back to the grassy field.

Quinn climbed off of the horse's back and ran towards the tiered fountain to wait for her friend. She called out to Aurora.

But no one came.

The only soul she saw was Mr. Larson. He was wandering around calling for someone, but Quinn couldn't make out the name.

"Mr. Larson," she called out to him.

"Quinn, are you back?" he came over and seemed confused to see her.

"I guess," she said. "But I don't see Aurora anywhere."

"I haven't seen my friend Reggie in years," he said.

"Years?" Quinn asked.

"Yes, I have been coming back here every day for three years now, but you're the first person I have seen in that entire time," he said. "How long did it take you to get back here?"

"I was gone for about three weeks," Quinn said. "I had to set up my trust."

"Three weeks?" Larson asked. "Tell me, did the pooka say that you failed at any of the conditions?"

"Yes," Quinn admitted. "I failed at faking my death. They had to search for my body."

Larson shook his head. "You should have taken longer to plan," he said.

"Why?" Quinn asked.

"I think this is the punishment for failing," he said sadly.

"What is?" she asked.

"We're trapped here, forever," he said. "Without getting to see the friend we made. Without getting to see the magical forest again. We're just trapped."

"That can't be right," Quinn said. "They wouldn't just leave us here. Aurora wouldn't just leave me here."

"But they did," Larson said.

"But why?" she asked. "To what end?"

"I don't know," Larson said sadly. "But there's no way home. Not that I've found anyway."

"So, we're just trapped here? Forever?" Quinn asked.

"I think so," Larson said. "There's no way home."

Quinn watched as Larson started to fade away.

"Larson? What's happening to you?' she asked.

But he couldn't hear her and he just disappeared.

Quinn started to panic. She didn't want to fade into nothingness like Larson did. She wondered if he was dead or if he would return.

She started towards what she thought the direction of the enchanted forest was and she walked for what felt like days.

When she thought she couldn't walk any farther, she saw the tiered fountain looming ahead of her. She had no idea how she had circled back to it.

She had no energy as she walked the rest of the way to the fountain. She felt completely drained of hope.

When she finally got back to the fountain, Aurora appeared and sat down next to her.

"What is happening?" Quinn asked Aurora.

"You weren't able to keep your end of the deal," Aurora said sadly. "So, we can't let you the rest of the way in."

"You mean, I'm just trapped here?" Quinn asked.

Aurora nodded sadly.

"Why did you come back?" Quinn asked.

"I wanted to see you," Aurora said. "It's against the rules, but I couldn't let you go on looking for me. You won't see me again. Not ever."

"Then why come see me at all?" Quinn asked.

"You seemed so nice," Aurora said. "I didn't want to watch you suffer."

"But leaving me here will make me suffer, don't you see?" Quinn said.

"No," Aurora shook her head. "You can end it quicker than that horrible Mr. Larson did."

"How?" Quinn asked.

"You must surrender to the despair and the sadness," Aurora said. "The creatures here feed on hope. They let you go when you don't have any more."

"What happens to me then?" Quinn asked.

"You just fade into nothing," Aurora said. "Just like Mr. Larson. Then you will finally be free of this place."

"So that's it?" Quinn asked. "Just give up?"

Aurora nodded.

Quinn broke down into tears, "I don't want to stay here. I want to go home."

"That's not an option anymore," Aurora took Quinn into her arms and whispered into her ear. "When you made your deal with the pooka, your fate was sealed."

Aurora wrapped her arms tightly around Quinn and started to sing a sad song. The music of her voice sent Quinn even deeper into despair.

Quinn cried into Aurora's shoulder until she faded away and disappeared.

BEAUTY AND THE THREE EVILS

THERE ONCE WAS A PRINCE named Jasper that ruled over a small province that his father had given to him. His father, the King, had sent him to care for this land and its people.

Instead of caring for them, the prince took advantage of them. He stole from them liberally; he drank and caroused. He often got into bar fights with unwitting townspeople and punished them and their families if they dared to fight back. He taxed them horribly and took what he wanted, when he wanted.

Everyone in his providence was afraid of him and his abusive power.

One day, a woman came to town.

She was the most beautiful woman anyone in the province had ever laid eyes on. She moved gracefully and spoke kindly to everyone she met. She was easy to talk to and everyone who spent any time with her related to her the woes of their province.

When she finally came across the prince, she walked up to him and introduced herself.

"I am Princess Ling, your father has sent me to oversee your governing of this province," she said.

"Princess?" Jasper said. "It looks to me like he has sent me a bride."

As Prince Jasper reached out for her, Princess Ling drew her sword from her side and caught him under the chin with the blade.

Prince Jasper stopped and raised his hand to his chin. When he pulled his hand away, he saw some of his own blood on his fingers.

Angered, Jasper drew his own sword and readied himself for a fight.

"I don't care if you are a woman," the prince said. "No one draws my blood and lives to tell about it."

The princess expertly stepped forward and disarmed the prince in a blur and knocked the prince to his back. Prince Jasper laid on the ground, in the dirt, his face alarmingly close to some pig dung.

He moved to rise, but Princess Ling stepped forward and placed the sword at his chin once again.

"My father will have your head," the prince said.

"Your father sent me here for yours," Princess Ling said.

"What?" the prince couldn't believe his ears. "My father would never have me killed."

The princess kept the blade of her sword pressed against Jasper's chin. "Your father is not pleased with how you care for his lands. He sent me here to take care of that."

The prince's heart fell. He couldn't imagine having disappointed his father so badly that the king had sent an assassin for his life.

"Please, what can I do to prove that I am a worthy caretaker and for my father to spare my life?" he asked.

Princess Ling stared down at him. "Do you really not know?"

"No," the prince begged. "Please tell me."

"All you have to do is speak to anyone in town," Princess Ling said. "There are three great evils that exist that make your towns-people's existence miserable."

"Please tell me," the prince said. "And I will take care of all of them."

"The first is the monster that lives in the lake," Princess Ling said. "It attacks when people are drawing water at the edge of the lake."

"I have heard of this monster," the prince said. "I will slay it and bring myself back into my father's good graces."

"It won't be good enough," she said.

"What is the second evil?" Prince Jasper asked.

"The second is the troll that lives in the forest," the princess said. "He abducts children and kills hunters searching for food."

"I will slay the troll as well," the prince said. "And what is the third, so that I may keep my lands and please my father?"

"The third?" the princess laughed. "You are the third, you fool. You mistreat your people. You overtax them and rob them. You beat them in the streets. You are the third evil."

The prince looked at the faces of the people who had gathered in a small crowd around him and the princess. He saw the faces of people who hated him, and faces that were full of hope that the princess would finish him off right then and there.

"Let me go to the lake," the prince said. "Let me prove my worth to you and the people of the town."

The princess withdrew her sword and allowed the prince to stand up. He picked up his sword and stared down at the princess as she stood near her.

"You have my word that I will defeat the monster in the lake," he said.

"And what of the other evils?" the princess asked.

"One at a time," the prince said.

Prince Jasper carried his sword down at his side and made his way towards the lake. The townspeople let him pass and then followed him down to the shoreline.

The princess followed him as well, and stood near the edge of the lake with her sword at the ready as the prince waded into the water.

The water rippled out ahead of the prince and then the water monster surfaced. It had over a dozen tentacles and rose up out of the water as it drew closer to the prince. He raised his sword and did a mighty battle with the monster in the lake.

The whole town watched as the prince rid them of the terrible monster that had been terrorizing them for years. They cheered when the monster finally fell and the current washed the body of the monster out to sea.

The prince waded back to shore, exhausted, but victorious.

The townspeople helped him back to the village and the princess followed. The people of the town helped to take care of the prince's wounds and brought him medicine, food, and water.

The princess watched as he grudgingly thanked the people who nursed his wounds.

When the prince was well enough, he rose early one morning and told the princess that he was ready for his second task.

Once again, the prince headed out with the people of the town following close behind. He headed into the forest, to take on the troll that terrorized hunters and stole children.

The princess stayed between the troll and the townspeople, but waited and watched the prince.

The troll came crashing out of the woods and the prince drew his sword.

After a mighty battle, where trees were felled and much blood was drawn, the prince defeated the troll and it lay dead in the woods.

The townspeople cheered once again and helped the prince back to the village. As they nursed his wounds and fed him willingly, he thanked them graciously and offered to pay for their services. He played with the children that brought him gifts and was polite and kind to everyone who visited him.

The villagers refused his offers of payment, telling the prince that defeating the two monsters was payment enough. But they were happy to visit the prince and offer their healing balms and nourishing soups. And the princess noticed that they were no longer afraid of him.

The princess waited for the villagers to leave for the day and went into the prince's room and sat on the edge of his bed.

The prince looked at her sadly and sighed.

"Why are you so unhappy?" the princess asked.

"Because I have to rid the town of the third evil," the prince said. "I am planning on throwing myself off of the cliffs above the ravine in the morning."

He took the princess's hand.

"Please tell my father that I am sorry for all of the misery I caused," he said.

Princess Ling shook her head, "You have already vanquished the third evil."

"What do you mean?" the prince asked.

"The townspeople love you, now that you have made their lands safe again," the princess said. "You no longer look at them as people to steal from and abuse."

The prince still looked ashamed, "But my father sent you to kill me."

The princess looked down at his hand that was still holding hers.

"I'm afraid it is my turn to be ashamed," she said.

"Why is that?" the prince asked.

"Because I lied to you," the princess said. "Your father and my father made a treaty. I was sent here to be your bride to seal their pact. When I got here, I saw how much you were hated, and I gave you these tasks in hopes of you dying and me not having to fulfil my part of the bargain."

The prince stared at her in silence as she spoke, but he never let go of her hand.

"I'm sorry," she said. "I'm sorry I lied. And I am sorry I tried to kill you."

The prince shook his head, "I should have already vanquished those monsters for my people. I don't blame you for not wanting to marry the monster you met when you came to town. But I am a new man now, that monster is vanquished as well. I wish that you would still do your part to fulfill our fathers' treaty. Not because you have to, but because you want to."

The princess looked at the prince and saw sincerity in his eyes.

"I will marry you," she said. "But not because of some treaty. I will marry you because I have fallen in love with the man who has become so gentle with his people."

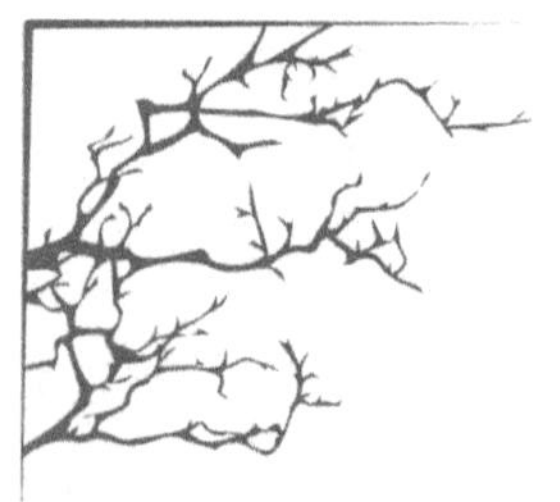

H.A.A.

THOMAS ENTERED THE room cautiously. It was a very small gymnasium that smelled of donuts and hot coffee and feet. It was also full of creatures he had never seen before.

There was a wood elf up at the front of the room. She was the most beautiful creature he had ever laid eyes on. Her long blonde hair hung down her back in flowing waves of gold. Her pointed ears peeked out through her hair and looked sharp enough to be a weapon. Her ocean blue eyes locked on his as he walked into the room.

Thomas knew all eyes were on him. He looked human. As far as he was concerned, he still was human. Mostly.

He could feel the eyes of the wood elf on him. She raised her nose into the air and sniffed, almost imperceptibly. She narrowed her eyes at him, but nodded just slightly. Her flowing green dress trailed behind her as she took her seat at the front of the room.

All of the creatures took their seats among the rows of folding metal chairs. Some sat on cushions near the front of the room. Some were eyeing Thomas as if they didn't trust him. But the creatures would look up at the wood elf and she would nod reassuringly at them.

The room settled into an uneasy silence as the wood elf raised her hand to quiet the room.

"My name is Aerin," she said. "For those of you who are new, I am a wood elf and I am the chair-fae in charge of running our meetings. I would like to welcome you all to this evening's meeting of Human Addicts Anonymous."

There were a few muffled claps around the room and then another awkward silence.

"I encourage all new-comers to speak at their first meeting," she eyed Thomas as she said this. "But if anyone else would like to get us started, it would be most agreeable."

She gracefully sat down on a wooden dining chair at the head of the group.

A small creature in brown overalls and a tiny bowler hat with a red glistening hummingbird feather sticking out of the band stood on his chair and cleared his throat.

"Ahem," he started. "My name is Alfrigg and I am a Human Addict."

"Hello, Alfrigg," chorused the room.

"I'm a brownie, you see," Alfrigg said. "And we tend to live with the humans. In their walls. In their homes. We see everything they do. We watch. We listen. We usually stay hidden. Completely unknown to the humans. But sometimes..."

Alfrigg stopped and took off his hat to reveal a small patch of wiry brown hair on top of his head.

"Sometimes, they discover us," Alfrigg looked ashamed. "And sometimes, they even try to make friends with us."

Alfrigg took a long pause before continuing, his voice sounded choked up as he spoke. "The last family I lived with. Their little girl discovered me. It started innocently enough. She left me milk and bread. The bread was so good. Homemade. Her mother was a bak-er."

Alfrigg shook his head in shame, "I started cleaning the kitchen at night. To earn my bread. You know how us brownies are, we feel bad just taking it from them, so we work. I didn't mind a little kitchen cleaning. I thought it was harmless. But then, on Sundays, the little girl would leave me a plate of honey. The good kind. Fresh from the farmer's market."

Heads nodded around the room in agreeing sympathy.

"I had to get out of there," Alfrigg said. "It was getting to be too much. I would feel compelled to vacuum and dust. I knew I had to leave when the little girl started leaving pieces of cake slathered with butter cream frosting. I found myself," Alfrigg paused to choke back tears. "I found myself cleaning their bathroom."

He sat down hard on his chair, wiping his eyes. The creature next to him patted him on the back and handed Alfrigg a hanky.

"Thank you, Alfrigg," Aerin said softly. "That was wonderful sharing. Anyone else?"

A manticore raised his hand and stood up.

"Hello, my name is Kallan, and I am a Human Addict," he said.

"Hello, Kallan," the creatures in the room said.

The manticore swished his tail out from under his feet and smoothed his hair back along his spotted head.

"I am a manticore," he started. "We are supposed to eat hu-mans. But I fell in love with one."

Everyone in the room gasped slightly.

"She wasn't supposed to be the one," Kallan said. "She was just wandering through the forest one day. I wasn't that hungry because I had just eaten a small troop of Boy Scouts. So, I kidnapped her, to save her for later. A midnight snack, maybe."

Kallan looked around the room and swished his tail again. "But she was so kind and gentle. She was never afraid of me at all. I just couldn't eat her."

Various creatures around the room nodded sympathetically.

"So, one day, I decided to let her go," Kallan said. "But she wouldn't leave. I knew it could only end badly. So, I left. I came straight here."

Applause burst out around the room punctuated by "Good for you." and "Good call." and "We're here for you."

Kallan sat back down and Alfrigg handed him his hanky. Kallan took it and blew his nose loudly.

A siren stood up suddenly, her beautiful blue hair cascading down her shoulders and back. Thomas could see the faint outline of iridescent scales on her skin.

"Hello, my name is Rhoswen," she said in a beautiful voice. "I'm a Human Addict."

"Hello, Rhoswen."

"I have such an addiction to humans that I can't even get into my own home anymore," she said. "I sing to the ships as they pass and they crash into the cliffs. My sisters and I would feed. Everything was fine. But I couldn't stop. I crashed every ship. They've all piled up around my home and I can't get in anymore. My sisters told me I have a problem, so I came here."

Another siren went over and took Rhoswen by the hand. She whispered something to the siren and they left together into a small side room where they could speak in private.

There was another awkward silence and then Aerin spoke up.

"How about you, our newcomer," she said. "Would you like to introduce yourself?"

Thomas looked around the room. All eyes were on him.

Thomas awkwardly stood up, suddenly feeling very unsteady on his feet.

"Hi, my name is Thomas, and I'm not sure if I am a human addict or not," he said.

"Hello, Thomas," some annoyed voices said.

"I mean, I was a human," Thomas said. "I am a human, most of the time. Until recently. Apparently, the dog that bit me last month was a werewolf. And now I'm not sure where I belong. I've been trying to keep my job, but things are different, you know. I'm changing."

"You're not a human anymore," a deep voice said from the back of the room.

Thomas turned to see another man at the back of the room. Thomas hadn't noticed him when he came in. The man must have slipped in quietly just before Aerin started the meeting.

He was mid-thirties and wearing jeans and a leather jacket. He wore dark brown work boots with the laces untied and his dark hair was slicked back.

"Who are you?" Thomas asked.

"I'm Warren," he said. "And if you'd like a sponsor, you just let me know. I'm a werewolf too."

"Well, I'm still human 29 days a month," Thomas said. "Like I assume you are."

Warren shook his head, "We're not human, not anymore. And if you think you are still one, then this is definitely the right place for you. Because that means you're an addict, just like all of the rest of us."

"But I'm still human," Thomas objected. "Mostly."

Heads shook all around the room.

"I'm not?" Thomas asked.

Kallan looked up at Thomas. "You're like me. You need a clean break. If you don't, you'll never kick the habit."

Alfrigg nodded, "Cold turkey man. Or you'll end up like the siren. Homeless. Destitute. Humans will do that to you. Whether you believe it or not."

Thomas looked over at Warren. "What did you do?"

"I found a pack," Warren smiled. "You can join mine. You might have to put up with a little hazing now and again, but I think you'll fit in just fine."

Thomas looked up at the wood elf. She nodded encouragingly at him.

"You need to be with your own kind," Aerin said. "You need to learn their ways."

"The humans will just reel you in and break your heart," Alfrigg said. "You'll be scrubbing toilets before you know it."

Thomas shook his head. "I can't just leave my life."

A small dragon had been sitting in the far corner of the room. He rose to his feet and showed Thomas a stump where one of his front feet was missing. "You see this, wolf?"

The dragon made eye contact with Thomas and held his gaze, just to make sure he was listening. Thomas stared into the frightening yellow eyes that loomed two feet above him and remained silent.

"This is what happens when you trust humans for too long," the dragon said. "I made a friend. A knight. He was all right. Friendly even. We were companions for years. But then someone claimed a dragon ate their sheep. The flocks were disappearing. And then that friend. That companion. He came for me. We fought. I got the better of him, but not before he took my arm."

Thomas stared at the stump that the dragon held out to him.

"This is what staying with the humans will get you," the dragon said. "Sooner or later, someone will find out your secret, and then they will hunt you. They always do."

The dragon blew two rings of smoke out of his nostrils and then turned and went back to his corner.

Aerin looked out the window at the moon and said, "That's wonderful sharing. Thank you everyone. But our time is almost up. Sunrise is coming soon."

The creatures stood and started helping the wood elf to put the chairs away, and in hiding all evidence that they had used the room.

Thomas looked from the dragon in the corner to Warren.

"Have you been hunted?" Thomas asked. "By humans?"

Warren nodded. He looked sad about it too.

Thomas sighed and walked over to the man standing in the back of the room.

"You have a pack?" Thomas asked. "They keep you safe?"

Warren nodded.

"I'll introduce you," Warren said. "Just talk to them. Then you can decide."

Thomas nodded.

He felt a hand on his shoulder and he turned to see the wood elf, Aerin standing behind him, her ocean blue eyes staring into his.

"You're making the right decision," she said in her soft voice. "And you're welcome back to our meetings anytime."

THE BURNING

It was a great honor to be chosen by the keeper of the burnings. It was also a terrible responsibility. If the keeper failed at his job, it could mean the end for the tribe.

Amka had been an apprentice for only a few days, but she was catching on quickly. She never wanted to be chosen, but now that she had, she enjoyed the looks of admiration from the tribe. From the other children. The bullies didn't dare even speak to her now.

Amka's mother had forced her to line up with the other children on the day of the choosing. She hadn't even wanted to leave the house that morning. It was especially cold and it was so warm and cozy under her favorite bear skin blankets. The faint smell of smoke and bear shank cooking for breakfast pleasantly greeted her first waking moments.

Her mother had pulled the warm blankets off of Amka and left her exposed to the cold that had permeated the hut through the night. She had gently pulled Amka to her feet and walked her over to where she had laid out Amka's clothes in front of the fire.

Her mother expected her to line up with the other children, now that she was of age. From the moment she turned twelve, her mother expected her to be chosen. She was the only one who had ever had any faith in Amka. Even her father didn't think Amka would be chosen. He was still asleep, snoring loudly in the next room.

Amka pulled on her clothes and bundled up as warm as she could. She was grateful that her mother had warmed her clothes by the fire before waking her. Her new boots waited for her by the hearth. Before Amka left, her mother smiled at her and kissed her forehead. She spoke traditional words of luck and blessings and hugged Amka before practically pushing her out the door and out into the shocking cold.

No parents were allowed at the choosing. Only the candidates, the chief, and the keeper.

Amka trudged out into the snow. It crunched under her feet as her new boots broke through the surface of the crisp white and crunched down through to Amka's knees. She hated when the snow got to the top of her boots. And this pair was too large and the cold wet started to seep down the tops of her boots, making her shins cold.

Deep snow also meant when the bullies shoved her down, she would not be able to see them again until after she got up. Losing sight of a bully meant additional surprise attacks, which was something Amka hated.

The sky was shimmering with greens and purples as the morning sunlight barely peeked over the jagged pointy tops of the pine trees in the distance. Amka looked out over the huge empty vastness that separated her village from the thick line of trees.

The only thing in the stark white emptiness were thousands upon thousands of small lanterns, all covered with a special tarp that only the keeper knew how to make. The tarp kept the wind and snow from extinguishing the lanterns.

It was the keeper's job to make sure that all of the lanterns stayed lit at night and remained in good repair. And it was the apprentice's job to learn the secrets to keeping them burning. As well

as the secrets to keep them from getting buried in snow through the night.

It was the keeper's job to keep the creatures at bay.

The last apprentice had been careless. The creatures had gotten hold of him. It was a common end for an apprentice. A new one was necessary.

Amka walked over to line up with all the other children in front of the chief and the keeper.

Tonraq, one of the boys who constantly bullied her, tripped her so that she fell face-first into the cold white, right in front of the chief and keeper.

All eyes were on her as she slowly got to her feet, her face stinging from the frigid slap to her face. She couldn't bring herself to look at the chief or the keeper. She was too ashamed to meet their gaze after such an embarrassing moment. The other children were laughing and their laughter echoed in the morning emptiness.

The chief ordered the children to be silent. But Amka was still too embarrassed to look up. It was all she could do to not cry. Her nose ran uncontrollably and she sniffed and wiped her nose with her sleeve, trying to keep her back to the other children. She couldn't imagine explaining to her mother what had happened. It would break her heart. The disappointment of Amka not being chosen would be too much.

The keeper walked over and stood in front of Amka. She stared at the tops of his boots. They fit him perfectly. There was no gap to let the snow trickle down to wet his shins. She found herself wondering if he had ever fallen face first into the snow. Or if he had a boy like Tonraq bully him when he was little.

She slowly lifted her eyes to the keeper to see if she could see any clue in his eyes as to whether or not he had been bullied, or if he had been the bully.

When she finally met his gaze, she saw a softness to his eyes. She could never imagine those soft brown eyes to belong to those of a bully. But she couldn't imagine anyone ever picking on him either.

He reached down to her and put his hand out, palm up. In his hand was the amulet of the apprentice. There was a large gouge out of one side with teeth marks punctured almost all the way through it.

He had gotten it back from the creatures. The amulet of the apprentice had survived the attack, even if the boy didn't.

Amka tentatively reached her hand towards the amulet. She had hoped this wasn't a cruel joke. She fully expected him to close his hand around the amulet and snatch it away from her at the last moment. But before she touched it, she looked up at his eyes once again.

There was no malice. No trickery.

She gently picked the amulet up, out of his hand, and stood in front of him holding the prize that all of the other children had wanted.

He smiled at her and then nodded to the chief.

The chief immediately gave the order for all of the other children to go home.

The apprentice had been chosen. And it was Amka.

She was so excited; she couldn't wait to go home and tell her mother. But she knew she wouldn't get the opportunity any time soon. Her mother would know the results before she arrived with the news. The other children filed back into the village to their homes.

Her mother would be waiting with her father on the front porch of their little hut. They would watch children around them go into their homes for breakfast. But Amka wouldn't be among them.

Her mother would be so happy. Her father would be shocked. But Amka would see neither reaction.

On the day of the choosing, the chosen one goes with the keeper to immediately start their training. Not home.

OUT OF ALL OF THE CHILDREN of her tribe, Panuk had chosen Amka to be his apprentice. Days later, Amka was still reeling from the choice. She had to run to keep up with Panuk's long strides in the snow as her short legs and too large boots and wet shins slowed her down during her lessons.

Panuk hadn't spoken to her about why he chose her. But he did give her instructions about what he needed her to do. They worked day and night, sleeping only when the work was done in the daylight.

At night, it was their busiest time. In the darkness, they tended the lanterns that divided the forest from the village.

Amka hated the nights. The darkness was vast and complete. The only light came from the lanterns. A small circle of light emanated around each one. She looked out across the lanterns at the tree line and watched for any movement. She had yet to see a creature.

She hoped against hope that she never would see one, but she knew that as the keeper's apprentice, it was inevitable. She would see one. The question was, would she survive it?

There was no moon. The sky was lit only by the stars and the purples and greens that shimmered above them all of the time. Amka was distracted by the tiny pinholes of light that were scattered in the sky like spilled rice.

Panuk nudged her and brought her focus back to the lantern they were repairing. Amka was grateful that he was gentle with her.

She had seen Panuk yelling at the last apprentice. When she asked him about it, Panuk told her his story.

His constant disobedience and arrogance were what got him killed. He didn't think he needed instruction, so he had ignored Panuk. He wandered too close to the tree line. He had wanted to see a creature. It was the last thing he ever saw.

Panuk had reassured her that there would be no yelling if she obeyed his every instruction. Safety was his main concern. For her and for the tribe.

Amka brought her attention back to the lantern. It was simply out of oil. It had been her job during the day to make sure all of them were filled and ready for the night.

Panuk reminded her that it was easy to miss a lantern during the day's rounds. He quietly reassured her that, in time, she would develop a pattern among them, so that none would get missed in the future.

He kept his voice soft and low in the darkness. Sound travelled across the vast white very easily. He did not want to draw the attention of the creatures.

When the lantern was filled and back to proper burning height, they covered it with the snow shade and stood up.

Panuk scanned the lanterns, looking to see if Amka had missed any others.

Amka saw it before Panuk. She lifted her arm and pointed to one of the farthest lanterns. It was almost to the tree line. And it wasn't lit.

Panuk sighed and looked down at Amka.

"You carry the supplies," he said. "Stay close."

Amka picked up their bag and slung it over her shoulder. The weight of it almost yanked her off her feet. She staggered two steps to the right and almost knocked over another lantern. She quickly regained her balance and ran to catch up with Panuk, who was already several of his long strides ahead of her.

She caught up to him and fell in line behind him. She could feel her breathing grow heavy and labored. Her shins were wet and frost was forming at the tops of her boots.

Panuk stopped walking and put his hand out to indicate that Amka should be silent. He scanned the tree line and stood frozen in place for a long moment.

Amka tried to calm her breathing. It was so loud in her ears that she could swear that the creatures could hear her breathing. She tucked her face sideways and pulled on the lining of her hood with her free hand. She breathed the warm humid air inside of her coat. She wanted to muffle her breathing so that the creatures wouldn't find them.

Panuk looked back at her and saw her with her hood stretched over her face to muffle her mouth. She grinned and shook his head, and then signaled for her to follow him again.

Amka let go of her hood and settled it back on her head properly and continued to follow Panuk. As they drew closer to the tree line, she could feel her heart beat louder and faster.

Fear gripped her chest. This was her first time this close to the trees at night. Only yesterday was her first time close to the trees at all.

Some of the children used to dare each other to go to the tree line during the day, when they could escape the eyes of the adults in the village. But Amka had never dared try. The stories of the creatures horrified her to her very core.

Her hands started shaking as they drew close. Her heartbeat in her ears was becoming deafening. Her breathing had become even more labored and Amka couldn't take her eyes off of the trees.

There were dark shadows hidden in the depths of the darkness. The lanterns lit up the edge of the tree line, causing shadows to dance back and forth across the black. She could only see a few feet into the trees, but she knew it was there.

She reached out to Panuk, to warn him.

He was watching the tree line ahead of the dark lantern. Amka was watching the tree line near the lit ones.

The shadows moved and danced unnaturally, not like the flicker of the flames, but like movement in the darkness.

Before Amka could make a sound, she realized that the *it* was a *they*, and they were everywhere.

Panuk had reached the lantern. But it wasn't out of oil. Amka would have been relieved that it wasn't her carelessness, but she was too frightened for relief when she saw that the lantern had been knocked over.

The broken lantern lay in pieces on the snow. The soapstone base smashed to bits.

Amka was too scared to speak, but she pulled on Panuk's sleeve with two weak jerks at his elbow.

He looked down at her and she pointed to the tree line.

"We're safe," Panuk said. "There's nothing there."

"No," Amka shook her head. Her voice was a strained whisper. "There's dozens of them."

Panuk looked back to the tree line. He squinted into the darkness and scanned the trees.

"I see nothing," he said.

Amka grabbed his sleeve once again and pulled him back.

Panuk suddenly sucked in a deep breath and placed his arm in front of Amka, gently pushing her behind him.

"Back up slowly," he said. "Don't trip over any lanterns."

Amka couldn't tear her eyes away from the tree line.

Slowly, the shadows started coming forward, out in front of the trees. When they were close enough for the light of the lanterns to hit them, nothing about them lit up except for their eyes.

An eerie yellow glow reflected back from the eyes of each creature. Amka started counting.

One, two, three, four...

Panuk continued to push her backwards.

Seven, eight, nine...

Amka stepped back slowly, she almost naturally steered around another lantern, and felt the warm glow of its light envelop her as she passed it.

Fifteen, sixteen, seventeen...

Her eyes had only made it halfway across the tree line as she counted.

A bell sounded behind her. Amka had never been so relieved to hear the ear shattering clanging of the tribe's warning bell. The watchers had seen Panuk and Amka backing away from the tree line and were ringing out the battle warning.

The village behind them started to light up and the men from the village were shouting and lighting torches from the fires along the village edge.

Before long, Amka could hear the crunching of footsteps in the snow behind her. There were so many torches coming up from behind her that she could feel the warmth of the fires cut through the icy chill of the night.

The warriors sped past Panuk and Amka and charged the tree line with shouts and fire and steel. Their swords had been dipped in the oil used in the lanterns and they had lit them aflame. Their war cries and their flaming steel were their only weapons against the shadowy creatures of the night.

Amka watched the eyes back away and disappear into the darkness once again.

Panuk grabbed her by the shoulder of her jacket near her hood and pulled her along, returning to the broken lantern. The warriors surrounded them while they hurriedly made a makeshift repair to the lantern. The base was shattered, but they could put a temporary replacement in its stead and it would light up and last until morning.

Amka worked fast, her hands shaking so badly that she almost couldn't be of any use.

Panuk did most of the work, but Amka was able to light the flame and gather their tools back into Panuk's bag.

As soon as they were finished, Panuk grabbed Amka by the arm and pulled her to her feet. He grabbed their bag and swung it effortlessly over his shoulder.

"Come with me," Panuk ordered.

He pulled her along beside him by her arm and she had to run to keep up.

Amka tripped in the deep snow again and again as Panuk pulled her along. His strong grip never let her fall, but her shorter legs wouldn't let her keep up. Panuk practically dragged her back to the village and didn't let go of her until they had passed the blazing war fires and were back to his hut.

Panuk pulled her inside and dropped his bag at the doorway.

Jissika, Panuk's wife, was waiting for them with a blazing fire and hot coffee.

Panuk pulled Amka over to the table by the fire and set her firmly down in a straight-backed chair. She felt off balance and confused. She didn't know what she did wrong, or why Panuk was so angry with her.

"How did you know?" he demanded.

"What happened?" Jissika asked.

Panuk looked directly into Amka's eyes. There was a fire in his eyes that was burning almost as hot as the fire in the stone fireplace behind her.

"How did you know?" he demanded again.

"There were," Amka swallowed. Her mouth was so dry that she couldn't speak. She tried to wet her mouth and tried again. "Shadows."

"What shadows?" Panuk demanded. "There was only darkness."

Amka shook her head. "There were shadows in the dark."

Panuk looked at his hands and realized he was gripping Amka's arms tightly. He released his grip and Amka could feel the blood flow return to her hands.

"She saved my life," Panuk looked over at Jissika.

"How?" his wife asked.

"She could see them," Panuk sat down on another chair and stared at Amka.

Jissika handed each of them a steaming mug of coffee.

Amka took it gratefully and sipped at the hot liquid. Jissika had made Amka's the way she liked it. With lots of sugar. The wetness returned to her mouth and the hot coffee cooled the fire that was choking down her throat. She savored the bittersweet flavor as she started to feel her hands relax from all of the shaking from fear and cold.

Jissika sat down on the other side of the table and quietly waited.

"What did you see, exactly?" Panuk asked.

"Are you angry?" Amka asked timidly.

Panuk exchanged looks with Jissika, who smiled softly at him and shook her head, and then looked back at Amka.

"I'm not angry," Panuk softened his voice. "I was forceful with you because I wanted you to stay safe. If I hurt you, I am truly sorry, but I did what had to be done in the moment."

Amka nodded and held her steaming mug tightly to her chest. She was starting to sweat inside of her coat.

As if reading her mind, Panuk pulled off his own jacket and gloves.

Jissika came over and gently took Amka's mug from her and helped Amka remove her coat and gloves. Amka immediately took the steaming mug back from the table and clutched it to her chest once again.

"I'm not angry," Panuk said softly, facing her knee-to-knee with their chairs. "I just want to know what you saw."

Amka shrugged, "I told you. There were shadows in the dark."

"That doesn't make any sense," Panuk sat back in his chair. "There are no shadows in the pitch black of that forest."

Amka stared at the hot brown liquid in her mug. A small bubble glided across the surface and it drew Amka's attention for a brief moment.

Jessika leaned forward onto the table and reached out for her husband's hand.

Panuk reached back and they interlaced their fingers on top of the table.

Amka watched without lifting her head. Her parents never showed each other the kind of affection she witnessed Panuk and Jissika express towards one another. Hostility ruled her home. But here, Amka felt comfortable.

"There are the legends," Jissika said.

"That's all they are." Panuk shook his head, "Legends."

"What legends?" Amka asked.

"Legends of the true keepers," Jissika said. "The naturals."

Amka looked to Panuk for an explanation.

Panuk shrugged and took a sip of his coffee. "There are legends that there are natural born keepers. They can see the creatures, they learn the trade faster, that sort of thing."

"Why haven't I heard the legend before?" Amka asked.

Panuk shrugged again. "Because there's no such thing. It's just a story."

There was a knock at the door.

Panuk rose and answered. The chief stood in the doorway and gestured for Panuk to step outside.

Jissika rose and handed Panuk his gloves and coat. He took them from her and put them on as he followed the chief outside.

"Should I go with him?" Amka asked, unsure of what she should do at the moment.

Jissika shook her head and sat down in Panuk's chair, facing Amka.

"Listen to me," Jissika said. "A natural could save the village."

"How?" Amka asked.

"A natural keeper can control the burning of the fire," Jissika said, almost in a whisper. "It is a long-forgotten magic, but it's still there."

"Where?" Amka asked.

Jissika pointed at Amka's heart, "I think it's in there."

Amka shook her head, "I don't have any family history of being a keeper. I'm the first."

"It doesn't matter," Jissika said. "It's not in a family line, it's in the keeper's heart. You have the heart of a natural."

"How do you know?" Amka asked.

"You're learning twice as fast as Panuk's best apprentice," Jissika said. "You've learned in days what took weeks and even months for the others."

Amka stared at the bubble that still floated at the top of her coffee.

"But I haven't survived as long," Amka whispered.

"Yet," Jissika smiled. "You saved Panuk tonight. No other apprentice has done that."

Amka shrugged, not knowing what to say.

"You need to learn to focus the magic," Jissika started.

The door flew open and Panuk came back inside. He was alone.

Panuk shut the door and took off his gloves and coat and threw them down to warm by the fire.

"The warriors have things taken care of for the night," Panuk said. "You need sleep. Tarkik is waiting outside to walk you home."

Amka nodded and slid off her chair. Jissika helped her into her coat and gloves and Amka and headed out into the frigid cold to be escorted home by a warrior.

WORD SPREAD QUICKLY in the village about what had occurred in the darkness the night before. The bullies no longer bullied Amka. In fact, they avoided her altogether.

Amka watched as Tonraq was playing with some other boys in the village. When Tonraq looked up and saw her, he stared at her with fear in his eyes. Before the other boys could notice, he casually suggested that they go play somewhere else.

Amka was left standing alone over a soapstone base with Panuk's tools in her hands. She knelt down on her work tarp and tried not to cry.

She could hear the girls in the village playing nearby. Amka wiped the tears away and continued her work. Panuk wanted more lanterns spread along the tree line before dark. The chief had demanded the front line doubled before nightfall.

Amka focused on her work, trying to drown out the loss of her childhood with her chores. She was to be the next keeper. Playtime was over.

Amka let her thoughts wander to what Jissika had said. There was magic involved with the making of the lanterns, but not much. She stared at the tarps that Panuk made to go over the lanterns. He infused them with magic so that they could withstand wind, snow, and whatever other harsh treatment the elements could throw at them.

Panuk's tarps could withstand a blizzard. She remembered back two winters ago, when there was the worst blizzard their village had seen in decades. Panuk's magic had kept the lanterns burning. And even more amazing, Panuk's magic had kept the lanterns on top of the snow as it piled up from the storm.

The snow had risen several feet over the course of the night, and the lanterns still remained lit and settled into the top of the snow.

Amka knew the keepers used magic. But as she worked, she wondered how much had been forgotten.

Panuk returned with the carcass necessary to make the oil they would use to keep the new lanterns burning and dropped it near Amka. She hated that part of the job. Without a word, she pulled out her knife and set to work.

By the end of the day, Amka and Panuk had set out twice the number of lanterns near the tree line than there was the evening before. It was their first line of defense.

Panuk and the chief were hoping that the extra light would keep the creatures at bay.

Amka watched the tree line while they worked. She saw no sign of the shadows dancing in the darkness. Just pine trees covered in a frosting of white.

When darkness fell, the lanterns were lit and the warriors were working out shifts for taking turns on watch. They didn't want to be caught off guard if the creatures dared to breach the light again.

Panuk and Amka stayed on watch as well. Amka was getting used to the long hours that were put in by a keeper. But it was mostly fear and adrenaline that kept her awake through the long nights.

That night, she felt especially awake in the early part of the evening.

Her eyes scanned the tree line, into the darkness. As the night drew on, there was no sign of the creatures.

Panuk sat by one of the war fires, helping to keep the fire watchers awake through the night. The whole village was lit up, as it would be if the bell had been rung.

Amka was nodding off by the fire several feet away from Panuk. It had been a long day and she felt sleep weighing heavily on her eyelids.

Panuk nudged her and handed her a hot cup of coffee. Amka took it and smiled sheepishly. Panuk grinned and walked back to the fire and the other men.

Amka took a sip of the hot black liquid. There was no sugar. She held the bitterness in her mouth for a moment and then swallowed, letting the heat of the mug warm her hands through her gloves.

Amka looked up across the vast white expanse filled with the yellow glow of the lanterns and into the darkness of the trees. She saw movement.

She stood up quickly, spilling her coffee onto the ground. Amka stared at the tree line intently, searching for shadows.

Panuk made a warning sound and all of the men fell silent.

Panuk walked quietly over to where Amka stood, and stared out to the trees where Amka was watching.

A line of warriors armed with flaming swords came and flanked Panuk and Amka.

"Should we sound the bell?" one of the men asked.

Panuk looked down at Amka, who was slowly walking towards the expanse of lanterns with her eyes fixed on the tree line.

"Sound it," Panuk said behind her.

Moments later, the bell was being rung and the metallic cacophony echoed out over the expanse of yellow glow.

Amka could hear the other warriors rising and running out to fortify the line.

She continued watching the trees and the shadows that were coming forward towards her. Their eyes started to glow in the light of the lanterns. But their bodies remained in shadow, even as they came into the light.

When they reached the front line of light, they each, one at a time, kicked over the lanterns, extinguishing them in the snow.

Warriors ran past Amka in full charge, their screams tearing past her like the gales of a strong winter blizzard. They had their fire and steel at the ready and they hit the tree line already swinging their weapons for battle.

Amka watched in horror as the creatures ripped through the warriors like they were nothing. Bodies of her fellow villagers lay on the snow, their blood seeping red into the stark white.

"Amka, come back," Panuk yelled from somewhere behind her.

Amka could feel the fires behind her flare into the full battle line. A wall of flames used only when the creatures broke the tree line. She had unknowingly crossed the line and was on the wrong side of the fires.

Something pulled her forwards.

Amka locked eyes with one of the creatures. It stepped on the body of Tarkik, the warrior who had escorted her home the night before, and creeped out deeper into the lanterns and their light.

She could hear the screams of her mother behind her, calling for her to come back. It sounded so distant and far away. Muffled like a dream.

Amka ignored the cries and kept moving forwards towards the creature advancing towards her. It was the alpha, and the other shadow creatures were closing in behind him.

Amka didn't take her eyes from the alpha. He was as big as Panuk's hut, and she could see its muscles tighten. Even up close, the creature was hidden in shadow. The light of the lanterns no longer had any affect. The alpha advanced on her and through the shadow of itself, she could see it ready to pounce.

Amka stared the creature in the eyes. She was so close to its face that she could see herself. Her own reflection in the yellow glow of the lantern-lit eyes.

Amka's mother screamed behind her, and Panuk desperately called her name.

She couldn't take her eyes off the creature. She felt hot, like she was standing in a fire herself. Amka started sweating under her coat and felt like her chest was on fire.

The creature suddenly stopped and stared at Amka with fear in its eyes. The type of fear when one realized that it has gone from being the hunter to the hunted.

The creature reeled back, but it was too late.

Amka focused the flames that she felt coursing through her veins and screamed with all her might from the pain. She threw her head back and let the fire out.

The creature in front of her burst into flames. Its screams shattered the silence in the forest and shook the trees.

The other creatures, all the way back to the tree line, exploded into flames and the pine trees that had lost their snow became unrooted and started to fall.

Amka, completely exhausted, fell face first into the snow.

She turned her head and looked into the eyes of the burning creature that lay in the snow in front of her. As her eyes closed, she smiled because she knew the creature was no longer a threat.

WHEN SHE AWOKE, AMKA didn't know where she was at first.

When her eyes came back into focus, she realized that she was in Panuk's hut. Jissika was sitting by her bedside checking a dressing that covered Amka's arm.

"What happened?" Amka asked.

Jissika smiled and leaned towards Amka and stroked her face.

"You're a natural," she whispered. "I knew you had it in you."

"What did I do?" Amka asked.

"You took control of the war fires," Jissika said. "It was amazing. The wall of flames behind you became your weapon. You set all of the creatures on fire and burned them to ash."

"Is it over?" Amka asked. "Are they all gone?"

The smile faded from Jissika's face.

"They're all gone now, right?" Amka was confused. "If I burned them, they're gone, right?"

"Not yet," Jissika whispered.

The door opened and Panuk came into the hut.

"She's awake?" he asked.

"Yes," Jissika looked over her shoulder at Panuk.

He came over and sat down in a chair next to the bed.

Panuk's face was serious as he looked down at Amka.

"Somebody please tell me what happened," Amka demanded.

She tried to sit up, but suddenly found herself in scorching pain. Amka pulled the bandage off of her arm and looked at her injuries for the first time.

She had severe burns going up both arms all the way from her fingertips to her shoulders. The burns followed the lines of her veins and were physically hot to the touch. She looked down and saw the same burns scorched across her chest.

Amka looked up at Jissika, whose eyes were filled with tears.

Amka reached her hands to her face and she could feel the same scarring reaching up her neck to her face.

She started to panic.

"It's okay," Jissika said. "Your burns are healing quickly."

"What?" Amka said. She felt like she couldn't control her breathing. She gasped for air as she tried to make sense of what Jissika said.

"Your burns, they were much worse last night," Jissika said. "You're healing. It must be a result of being a natural."

Amka looked at Panuk. He stared at her like he had never seen her before.

"I'm so sorry I chose you," he said.

Amka felt like she had been shot through the chest by one of the hunter's arrows.

"How could you say that?" she asked.

"You being chosen, it activated your powers," he said. "The creatures are drawn to you, just as you are drawn to them. When I chose you to be my apprentice, I put you in extreme danger."

"But I can end this," Amka said. "We know I can burn them. And I can heal."

Panuk looked at Jissika and then back to Amka.

"It's not that simple," he said.

"Why not?" she asked.

Panuk sighed heavily and looked at Jissika once again.

"She must see it," Jissika said softly.

Panuk stood and started to put on his coat.

"Come with me," he said.

Amka rose from the bed and followed Panuk outside.

Jissika followed behind her carrying Amka's boots and coat.

Amka didn't feel the cold or the snow.

As she walked outside, the snow melted for several feet around her as she walked.

Amka walked on bare ground for the first time in her life as she stepped out of Panuk's hut and walked through the village.

Everyone around her stopped what they were doing as Amka walked past. Children started to cry when they saw her. Even Tonraq stepped away from her in fear.

Amka made her way around Panuk's hut and to the edge of the village, where she could see out across the vast expanse of white that used to lead to the forest.

Instead of the jagged pine trees that lined the edge of the forest, there was nothing but ash. The location of the trees and the creatures were only marked by ash and blackened scorch marks on the ground.

Amka made her way across the expanse. Hundreds of lanterns lay crushed and extinguished in the snow.

Amka ignored the jagged pieces of soapstone that lay scattered around her. The snow melted in front of her and the water steamed up from the baked dry ground beneath her feet.

She carved a path through the expanse and to the tree line. She never once took her eyes off of what lay ahead of her, now exposed to the light of day. The trees of the forest lay on the parched earth, crumbling into ash as she walked past them.

As she made her way into the remains of the forest, she saw what had worried Jissika and Panuk.

A huge cavernous hole stood in the middle of the forest. It was as tall as any tree that would have been hiding it. It looked like the mouth of a cave, except for the fact that there was nothing around it. Just a black hole standing in what was left of the forest.

Amka felt drawn to the opening.

She walked closer to it and examined it from close range. It was nothing but pitch black.

Amka looked back towards the village. A crowd had gathered to watch her. The entire village crowded into the expanse, but remained close to the village. Mothers held their children close. The remaining warriors held their weapons ready and were keeping the war fires burning.

She searched their faces until she saw her parents standing with Panuk and Jissika. They were at the front of the crowd, almost dead center.

Amka turned back to the black hole and reached out to it.

It stood silent, black, still. Until she touched it.

As soon as Amka's fingers touched the black, a shrill scream filled the air. It brought Amka to her knees with her hands covering her ears.

When the shrieking stopped, Amka looked back at the villagers. They had been covering their ears and cowering from the sound as well.

Amka met Jissika's eyes across the expanse.

She remembered Jissika's words.

A natural could save the village.

Amka turned to face the black hole in front of her. She summoned up all of the strength she had left and focused on the hole.

The villagers shrieked behind her as the war fires shot up high into the sky and then came back down to earth. The flames scorched their way across the expanse, drawing more power from each lantern that remained burning as it passed.

Amka focused the power of the flames through the black hole. She could feel herself burning, but remained focused on the vast darkness of the hole.

The war fires shot through into the darkness and carried her with it, through the hole and into the black. She could feel herself dying. The power of the darkness was too much for her on her own.

But suddenly, there was a second surge of power. The flames increased and Amka felt like she was having a second wind. She focused her mind once again and directed the flames into the darkness. When she felt the flames no more, she blacked out and fell to the earth.

All Amka could feel anymore was cold. There was no darkness, only white. And the feeling of being drawn by some inexplicable force was gone.

Amka opened her eyes, expecting to see the shimmering purple and greens of the sky. But instead, she saw her father's face.

He reached his hand out to her to help her to her feet. He wasn't wearing his coat or his gloves.

She looked at his arm and saw the burns that followed the veins up his arm to his shoulder.

Amka stared at her father with amazement, "You?"

Her father nodded. She took his hand and he pulled her to her feet.

Her burns matched his, almost exactly. The signs of a true natural. The burnings that indicated that they had the power to keep the creatures of the darkness at bay.

The creatures would be back. They always found a way. But the next time, the naturals would be ready.

Don't miss out!

Visit the website below and you can sign up to receive emails whenever Judy Lunsford publishes a new book. There's no charge and no obligation.

https://books2read.com/r/B-A-LRKI-XOKPB

BOOKS 2 READ

Connecting independent readers to independent writers.

Did you love *Magic From the Dark*? Then you should read *The Wild Hunt*[1] by Judy Lunsford!

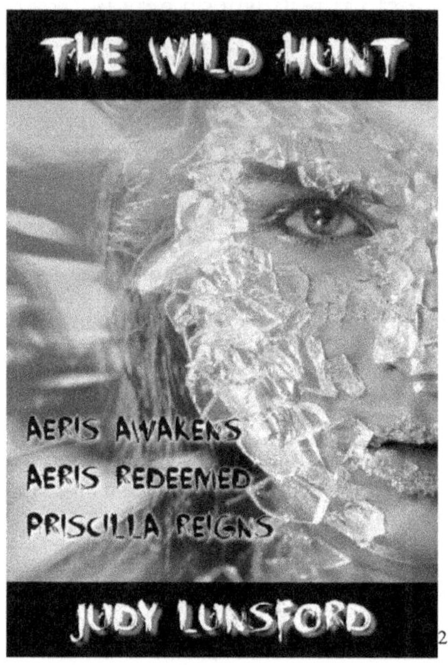

[2]

All three of THE WILD HUNT short stories in one place. *** AERIS AWAKENS -- Eli dreams of living in a fantasy world where he is a warrior and a leader. But in reality, he just works in retail. Until one night... *** AERIS REDEEMED -- Aeris returns to track down his memories. But finds something else entirely. -- Follow up short story to Aeris Awakens. *** PRISCILLA REIGNS --Priscilla is Queen of The Wild Hunt. But with the Ice King's followers against her, how long can she maintain her reign? Short story #3 of The Wild Hunt series.

---

1. https://books2read.com/u/mYp5wM

2. https://books2read.com/u/mYp5wM

Read more at https://linktr.ee/judyl.

Also by Judy Lunsford

Bird Lady
The Bird Lady
The Bird Lady: 10th Anniversary Special Edition
A Very Birthday Christmas
Seeds of Today: The Bird Lady Wedding

Crystal Tower
Rumtuskin of the Emberdiggers
Seeking Garille

Fire Lily
Fire Lily
Bezbell
Kirog
Shandoah

Gamers
Gamers
Runners
Schemers

Joshua Fahlstrom
Reality Fails
Fahlstrom's Library
Shade

Judy's Journal
Judy's Journal
Judy's Journal: Winter 2020
Judy's Journal: Autumn 2020
Judy's Journal: Christmas 2020

Letters from Alexia
Letters from Alexia, Volume #1, Sally and the Buccaneers

Moon Songs
Moonlight Magic

The Wild Hunt
The Wild Hunt
Aeris Awakens
Aeris Redeemed
Priscilla Reigns

Trunk of Alexia
Sally and the Buccaneers
Sally and the Marauders
Sally and the Sorcerer

Standalone
The Autumn Fairy and Shadow Tail
Moon Songs
The Moon and The Moths
Airship Pilot Waffles
The Monster Bed
The Magic Pond
Life Unscripted
Trunk of Alexia
Fairy Short Stories
My Fairy Godmother Wears Biker Boots
The Rule of Three
Again Upon a Time
The Dollhouse

The Tank
The Dragon's Lair
Siren Bound
Luna's Adventure
Crafting Christmas
Fantasy Faire
The Red Dart
Alien Dreams
The Cat
Finding Ms. Blackwood
Story Hoard
The Sea Journal
The Butterfly Boy
PlantMan662
Shadow Mountain
Pooka Deals
The Red Dart, Special Edition
Beauty and the Three Evils
First Stories
H.A.A.
The Burning
The Secret Gondal Society
Monster Party
Magic From the Dark

Watch for more at https://linktr.ee/judyl.